Love's Darkest House

by

Ginny Lynn

Love's Darkest House

Cover Art by *Diana Carlile*

The Wild Rose Press, Inc.
PO Box 708
Adams Basin, NY 14410-0708
Visit us at www.thewildrosepress.com

Publishing History
First Black Rose Edition, 2018
Print ISBN 978-1-5092-1956-8
Digital ISBN 978-1-5092-1957-5

Published in the United States of America

"Let's see if you can stop this, my dear.
Now we test your will and see if you can feel more than my strength against yours with my lust riding across your delicate skin."

I dared not open my eyes as I didn't want to see him in this way. Not with seduction on his wicked tongue. I pleaded for myself to wake up. Wake from this dream that had grown out of simple chemistry for a sexy male. Wake from the temptation which dared to happen. Wake and break the spell before I was a sleeping victim of this want and desire. But all I felt was the press of his lips as the thunder rolled across our bodies.

Such an innocent touch was deceiving. The kiss grew like the air that rolled the center of the storm over us. I had become the central area where the line separated dark from light and prey from predator. I knew which I was and it scared me but not enough to shock me awake. He leaned into me as he pulled my arms to my sides, increasing the amount of our bodies touching. As his arms crept along my ticklish waist, I was yanked the last bit against him where my breasts were a mashed ripeness against his ribs.

Kudos for Ginny Lynn

2012 WETA Awards Winner
in Paranormal category

Dedication

To my Renaissance Friends:
Melissa, Michelle, Angie, Melinda,
Karen, Michele, Brittani, and Kim
Keep reading, dreaming, and flying.

Chapter One

As someone who had made a living off breathing life into vintage items, my eyes appreciated the grand beauty of the home in front of my wheezing car. With the chilled air tossing bronze leaves around, I feared the inside of the dwelling would hold no inner warmth for me. I whispered a prayer of thanks that my junker of a car had made the six-hour journey and pulled out the letter that had brought me to this small southern town. The first of three correspondences that had changed the course of my life in the last month. After the passing of my step-grandfather, I came to be the sole inheritor of the sixteen-acre estate and all its contents.

Dank and inky dark outside, a single burning candle left a subtle light in the front window. Did a housekeeper wait at this late hour? The attorney informed me someone would be at the house to let me in. I appreciated it as I hated the idea of walking into an unfamiliar gothic estate alone at this hour. But why a candle and not a front porch light left on to show my way into the quiet house? It may have looked more in time with the aged flavor of the house, but it didn't make me feel the security a lit candle was rumored to induce.

The slightly crumpled paper in my shaking hands had come from Mr. White. He had been the Fenmore family attorney since fresh out of law school. The few words penned had been recited enough times to have it memorized.

As the last living member of both family lines, you would be required to stay at the estate for a few days as you make your decision on accepting the terms of the will as written by Mr. Fenmore after your grandmother's tragic heart attack.

Being in a place I had never even seen, other than in pictures, left me with an awkward sense of being an outcast. But after losing my job to a buyout along with most of my newfound independence, I desperately needed a home to call my own.

My thin trench coat wasn't substantial enough to withstand anything under forty degrees. The frigid air made me shiver in my worn denim jeans and simple long-sleeved blouse. But I hesitated a moment to gather enough courage to step up to the imposing thick wooden front door with its enormous lion knocker at eye level for the average adult.

Average, that described me in a nutshell, except for the visions. Those had ruined my chances of already being married as my last doozy had been when a gentleman caller attempted to kiss me goodnight. It had resulted in me screaming at my internal screenplay as his cool lips had brushed across mine before I fainted. Thank God, he had revived me before he'd run for the hills.

I still beat my head against the wall of that particularly embarrassing moment in my loveless life. I'd tried to pinpoint my triggers, but the only things they had in common were emotions and anxiety unless you counted random timing. My visions had become frequent enough that sex hadn't been attempted in over three years. I was even afraid to head into a sex-toy shop as I might have an episode in the swing aisle.

Reaching a trembling hand to the cold steel knocker, I jumped when the door shook with wind and age as my fist rapped a tone throughout the wind-filled doorway. I stepped back just as the door shuddered with the effort of someone pulling it open. My heart leapt into my tight throat as the door creaked open a sliver more. I paused for a second and saw no one visible in the breath of drafty space that sucked at me from the gloomy foyer.

"Um, hel-lo?" I stuttered the question, waiting for someone to pop up in my line of sight.

No reply, not even a scuttle of feet to prove someone had physically opened the ancient door. A stiff breeze pushed me into the open alcove, almost toppling me onto the white marble floor.

"Is anyone here? Mr. Wh-White?" My thumping heart beat against my ribcage as I straightened up.

A screaming whirl of wind outside sucked the door shut with a window-rattling shake and snuffed out the candle in the window.

"Can I help you, ma'am?"

I squeaked at the baritone voice that rose from the encompassing blackness in front of me. When my vision adjusted to the lack of light, an over six-foot tall, willowy shape stood in the shadows. My mouth went dry. In the instant it took to gulp down my surprise, he stepped closer and struck a match. I jumped but he was only lighting the candlestick in his large hand. The hand led up to a face which made me gasp with a whole new feeling. He was beautiful. Men weren't usually described in such a manner, but this specimen had a lean body, dark hair, and eyes as mesmerizing as sherry topaz in the light of the burning flame he held. The flickering emphasized his high-cut cheekbones and elegant nose.

"Save him," whispered in my head and then disappeared. What the hell was that? Scrutinizing the vacant space, no other person came forward to claim those cryptic words clinging like ice to my spine.

"Where did you come from, and why were you hiding behind the door?" I rambled while I pulled myself back together.

"You knocked on the door and proceeded to walk right in, so I should be asking who you are?"

"No, I didn't open the door. You did."

"I assure you, ma'am, I did not open the door. And who you are still remains unanswered."

"If you were the one with the duty to stay up for me, then you would already know who I am."

He sighed deeply, almost blowing out the candle in his still grip. "Let's say I'm a man of caution where damsels are concerned. Your name, please?"

"I'm Renata Barkely, granddaughter of the Fenmores, and Mr. White wrote for me to be here."

He nodded his head and said, "Yes, Mr. White told me a member of the family would be arriving before sunrise. Sadly, he wasn't forthcoming with any details other than it being due to the reading of the will."

I stared at him and waited.

"Do you have any bags?" he asked, his tone cool and nonchalant.

"Yes, there is one in my car."

"If it's unlocked, and you're willing to hold this candle for me, then I'll retrieve it for you."

4

In the absence of a valet service, and this guy being a complete stranger, I refused to stay in an unfamiliar house as he rummaged through my few belongings.

"I appreciate the offer, but I'll grab my stuff and be right back in. I'd be grateful if you continued holding the light while I make my way back."

"Of course, we wouldn't want any blood spilled on this white marble," he responded with a hint of a smirk on his handsome face.

The situation turned creepier by the minute. I stumbled out the door and jogged to my car. For a fleeting moment, I thought to drive out of there as if my life depended on it. I might put that plan into action, depending on how the next few moments played out. Slipping my cell phone out of my battered hobo bag, I dialed the number in the letter from Mr. White's office. Yes, it was after hours but I prayed someone would pick up so I would have some type of knowledge of what I had stepped into. It seemed as if a presence weighed on the estate, like a thick layer of moss after the rainy season.

"You have reached the voicemail for Mr. White, attorney at law. Please leave a message at the sound of the tone and he'll get back to you during business hours. Thank you."

"Mr. White, it's Renata Barkely. Can you call me back on my cell phone when you get in the office, or when you check your messages? I'm at the estate with questions that need answers."

I clicked off and wondered what to do next, then realized I had nowhere to run. I had nothing. I was destitute, penniless, and a shell of the passionate woman I had once been. The only light in this tunnel would be to at least stay here for the few days I committed to and happily accept the $5,000.00 stipend to walk away from all of this southern grandeur. Then I would run for the hills as I recreated my future. The problem was dealing with the next few days of uncertainty to get to the goal line. Did I want to put myself through this? No. Was it the only way to get back on my feet? Possibly.

The earlier whisper of power returned to hum in my ears again. Jerking to see who might be around, I scanned for anyone playing games with me.

"Who are you?" I questioned of the rustling wind as it brushed me like a body in a crowded hallway.

"Go. Save him."

Reaching out for the firm steel of my old car, I let the chill of it sink into me as did the recognition. The husky voice belonged to my grandmother. *Shit!* I was losing my mind. There was no way my grandmother would choose to visit me now. She'd been dead from a heart attack almost a year now.

"Renata, save him."

"Granny?" I forced out the question, not believing myself.

A cloud of warmth enveloped me, like walking through a sauna, and honeysuckle wafted through the thick air. That erased my doubt about it being her, and she needed me to help someone. She had told me years ago that my visions were only the beginning of what else was truly out there for the spirit to conquer. Her body did not rest here, as there were no available plots in the old cemetery on the estate but her spirit had lingered. Had she been waiting for me? Something told me to see what she needed. She had been there for me, and I would do the same for her, especially since I had been taking my college exams when she left this earth. Pulling up my big girl panties, I rolled my college dorm cart back to the dimly lit doorway.

I stifled my surprise that he stayed inside the house as I knew he had heard me approach with the wheels bumping along the walkway. There he stood, just where I'd left him, as if frozen in that moment of my internal conflict with his lack of chivalry. Had a pause button finally been installed in my life? Strangely, it seemed fitting as I took in the items around us—an array of vintage furniture, worn Persian rugs, and a true grandfather clock ticking away the dusty time.

I shouldn't have jumped when he spoke, but my nerves were in worse shape than my checking account.

"Seeing as how you're here, and I'm awake, I'll show you to your room. Do you have any requests, demands, lovers on their way to join you?"

"I'm low maintenance but a clean bed and a fluffy pillow would be acceptable. No one will be arriving other than Mr. White when he has the paperwork for me to look over. What's your name and what do you do here?"

"I'm Kenrick Giles, and my normal title is caretaker, but some would call me the ghost of the property." The last part came with a look of pure mirth.

"And why are you escorting me around with a candle? Is there a power outage in the area?"

His chuckle was sexy as it hung in the air. "No, ma'am, Mr. Fenmore didn't believe in fluorescent lighting and refused to have any installed when he took possession of the house. The hum they created would annoy him to no end. He was typical of his age as he and Mr. White used to both bicker over the annoyance of modern technology being more of a burden than a gift."

"He could have used incandescent lights or did he not know about those?"

Kenrick continued leading me around the house, but he would turn to face me when he was answering my questions. "I tried when hired, but he claimed to be too set in his ways to need them. He was the type of man up at sunrise and headed to bed at sunset. Your grandmother was the only person who could talk him into any newer comforts, but he had a limit to what he would tolerate in his home. Mr. White finally succumbed to using a cell phone, but he won't answer it unless he knows who is calling him. I can give you that number, if you'd like it?"

He began walking away as he spoke, leaving me to stand by another grandfather clock. I looked into the face of the clock and wondered which was more personable, the man or the beautiful clock. Both seemed lovely and useful but daylight would show any flaws. I sighed deeply and rolled after him. I knocked around the unlit rooms as I fought to keep up with the man gliding round items like a modern-day wraith. His body bent around furniture I didn't see until I was upon it. Did he have wonderful night vision or had he memorized every room in the sprawling house?

"Excuse me? Do you mind slowing down or at least giving me the light so I can see what's about to eat me?"

I heard a sexy chuckle in response as I passed through another doorway and ran into him.

"*Oof.*" The air rushed out of my chest at the abrupt

halt against the man in front of me. The candle went out in the whoosh of air from my lips.

There I was, against a hard male body, in a room that surrounded us like a dark shroud. My body shivered as a comforting sensation surprised my trembling skin. A change in air pressure was tangible, as if a hand pushed at my back. Feeling a breeze coming upon me as he quickly stepped back, I felt oddly cold again as if he had taken all the warmth with him when he'd torn himself out of my personal space.

Hearing a match scratch to life, the flame carried to the candle where it illuminated the interior of a bedroom lost in time. The walls were an undetermined green with whitewashed moldings and a cream-colored marble fireplace on the back wall. In the middle sat a four-poster bed, and there was a small seating area in front of me with a deep green velvet love seat and high back chair. I couldn't see all of the details as he only had the single light for me to peruse by. He set the candle on the worn surface of the white side table and then reached for the clear oil lamp on a single long bookshelf in between the tiny areas. Once he had the flame at full height, my eyes could make out the sage of the hand-painted wallpaper and the embroidered pillows along each stuffed piece of furniture and against the whitewashed headboard. Somehow, the room held the poise and delicacy of the female spirit.

A thin trace of dust covered the room's belongings but it could never hide the vintage beauty of the room. I moved to run my hand across the cream and black damask fabric of the comforter. The pillows on the bed were of various sizes and covered in an array of black and mint satins. Soon I would be able to crawl into the inviting space, but for now, I glanced over the items on the bureau. There were a few sepia landscape photographs that I guessed were taken around the property when the house had been much younger, maybe in the early 1900s. I picked up his discarded candle and moved on to the marble fireplace with its clean hearth and the lady's vanity with wrought iron chair and large oval mirror. The fabric seat of the iron chair held a leaf-design tapestry and looked original. All the pieces were in better shape than they should be, for their age, but maybe my step-grandfather had paid someone to restore the pieces to what would pass for mid-1800 styling. It would have no bearing on what would be happening over the next few days, but I would get around to asking questions once I saw what could be listed as a change to my immediate future.

Hearing steps on the creaky wood floor reminded me I was not alone in the room I had been concentrating on.

"As you can see, many upgrades have been made to improve comfort and carefully mixed with the vintage style of the house. This is the only bedroom on this floor with its own bathroom that's why I chose it for you."

Why did it seem so intimate for this man to pick out what he thought would fit my needs? A blush warmed my cheeks as I gazed at his face while the thought sank in. A sudden flare of pain shot across the webbing between my right thumb and finger distracting me. Biting my lip, I quickly put the candle down on the closest hard surface and brought my hand up to see what I had done to it. Kenrick was suddenly next to me and took my hand in his as he used the light from the tall hurricane lamp to have a closer look.

"Be still for a moment, you have wax cooling against your skin. I'll peel it off," he stated softly before I could even protest.

Delicately, he used the edge of a fingernail to slip the cream drop of wax away from my tender hand.

"There doesn't seem to be a blister forming but let's rinse it under some cool water to make sure." He began walking me toward the bathroom and its décor of matching green tones with white and black accents.

My sense of smell picked up the subtle scent of the well water just before he gently dunked my hand under the cold stream from the ornate faucet. Seeing a flash in my peripheral vision, I quickly glanced up to see amber eyes in the small framed mirror in front of me. Swiveling my head to the right, I was so close to Kenrick that it became clear it was his eyes staring at me in the gilt-edged glass.

"Your freckles are adorable," he said to me as we huddled so close.

"Um, thanks," was all I could manage.

"There must be something you have to say because you keep staring at me," he prompted.

"I'm sorry. That was rude of me." I averted my eyes back to the slight pink tint which just happened to form the shape of a heart on my hand.

"A heart?" I whispered.

"Yes, I have one," he answered with a quirk to the corner of his mouth.

"Pardon me?"

"You were wondering if I had a heart and I do," he explained, as the grin grew cocky.

I scoffed at him. "Well, of course you do."

Shrugging his shoulders, his face inched closer to mine. "What else do you want to know?"

With that, I noticed my hand felt warmer in his grip, and it wasn't even cooled by the tap water. Staring into his eyes, I had no idea what to say. When his thumb caressed my wet one, I shivered. "I think it's okay to take it out of the water now."

No emotion came across his face as he replied, "It can stand a moment more."

"I'm fine, Kenrick."

"Yes, you are."

The blush returned and he was close enough to see it this time. What if he tried to kiss me? How would it feel to have those luscious lips on mine, if even for a brief second? Why the hell had I even thought that? Awkwardly, I jerked myself out of his hold and away from the temptation which had slithered into me. "Not even knowing you, I find you're an exasperating flirt. Are you normally like this?"

"No one usually insults me to my face." A light entered his eyes.

"Well, there's a first time for everything." I couldn't fight the smile taking the place of my frown. "I'm tired. Is there anything else that needs handled while we wait for Mr. White?"

"Unless you need a particular thing handled, then I'll just offer to show you the grounds in the light of day tomorrow."

"I appreciate the offer but I don't want to take you away from any duties you need to perform." It came out as more concerned than with the bite I had intended it to carry.

"Ms. Barkely, soon you will see I never turn away

from my duties when there is something that needs my full attention. Good night and pleasant dreams."

He shut the door and when he did, a breeze ran through the room. It was as if it had to follow in his footsteps. I hoped I had imagined that.

Chapter Two

I was on edge, like being so close to the cliff's edge one breath was the difference between admiring the view or becoming part of it. After changing into my worn but favorite cotton pajama set, I forced my tense body to slide under the elegant paisley sheets and started counting sheep. I'd already tried using my excess energy up by unpacking but it hadn't relieved the apprehension that an invisible presence in the room watched me. The one Victorian painting made me wonder if I needed to check for peepholes in the faces of the gentry in any portrait I came across in the manor. That brought a cold realization where my fear and paranoia were getting the best of my normally sensible character.

The clicking of the mantel clock was slower than the thumping of my heart so I focused on slowing the beat to a more relaxed tempo. Being like this on my first night was not a good sign of the days to come. If I didn't calm down soon, then the visions would kick in where my heart beat left off. Rationalizing the matters of the day was a way for me to dissect them into manageable pieces. If that didn't work then jogging up and down a flight of steps might exhaust me into not caring how bad my nerves wanted to crawl away.

Yes, I was in an unknown place with an attractive man who might have an underlying plan once the attorney read the will stipulations. Did he have hopes that he was in the bequest or was he just a type of butler who helped out my step-grandfather? That image made me smile a bit. Did he know I was getting a few thousand for even showing up for the will and it made him believe I was nothing but a spoiled gold digger? Why the hell did I care? He was no one to me. I'd gladly walk away from this insanity now rather than subject myself to enough drama that my visions were more frequent than prime time commercials.

The fuzzy sheep in my head were jumping over the ticking clock as I forced myself to clear enough tension to somewhat meditate. Those rules about unruly kids just needing to lie down for a few minutes; I was totally that kid in my head. After all of the anxiety attacks with impending visions, I had to go to a yoga expert to help me learn to meditate. It had helped a great deal during the past year, even if I had to clean her house to pay for my sessions. The money had dwindled after we'd gotten familiar with each other so she'd offered a barter system as I was about out of funds by the fifth session. My pride allowed me to accept her offer and I had thanked God for it.

I pictured myself pushing storage boxes out of my cranium as a way to get myself centered. It was a silly image to use but I'd come across it in a yoga textbook and had successfully tried it out during the fourth lesson. She'd laughed at how fast I calmed my twitching, so I shared it with her afterward. I pushed aside a large purple tote which had Kenrick written on it, but it pushed back. Mentally frowning, I rolled up my pajama sleeves and shoved as hard as I could muster for such a small image. I succeeded in making it skitter across the floor of my mind and dusted my hands off before going to the next bin. The instant I concentrated on it, the cube turned into an orange one with Kenrick's name scribbled across it. No way.

Kicking it like a soccer ball, it slid into place by the purple one. Eyeing them carefully over my shoulder, I went for the biggest green one. A bright emerald green tote but when I went to position it beside the others, it turned into a copper bin, the color of Kenrick's eyes. Shit. I hadn't registered the clock ticking anymore so I knew I must have halfway hypnotized myself for the images to change so quickly. I squealed as the bin glowed so bright I had to shield my eyes from the intensity of it. Then came a soft chuckle, making me jump in surprise.

Kenrick stood before me, just inches from touching me. I was still in my ice cream cone fabric pajamas, but he wore jogging pants. How had my brain envisioned him to look so sexy in a pair of faded olive jogging pants? What the hell was going on in my disturbed mind? I'd never had it turn this way before. The technique never involved actual people, let alone strangers, that was part of the reason for meditating in the first place. Unnerving but worse as he began smiling at me like I was missing something.

"What? And why are you here? I don't recall inviting you into my dream." I tapped my foot.

"But you did."

"The hell I did!"

"*Tsk, Tsk*, what language from such a soft woman."

"Excuse me? Soft?" I'd been called mousy, timid, and serious but never soft. Maybe it was the pajamas or the fact I'd taken my hair down from its messy updo after the drive over. I hated having it all in my face when stressed, even if it hid the frown which always landed between my dark eyebrows.

"No insult intended, my lady," was his only reply as he gave a more neutral expression.

"I need sleep and you aren't a part of that, so you can be on your way now," I emphasized with a shooing motion of my hands.

"Sadly, I'm not that easily dispatched. And what would make you think I'm here to facilitate your sleep?" The look on his face put a different meaning to the words.

"I may be dreaming but it's my mind you've hopped into so I should be able to call the shots here. That would mean you taking your tight butt out of my safe place and back to wherever you came from."

He stood there with his hands behind his back.

If he wouldn't leave then I could try to. I walked to the other side of my mind and envisioned a door farthest away from my intruder. I practically jumped through it and instantly felt myself falling into deep space. Just as I opened my mouth to scream myself awake, a pair of strong arms caught my body. Sighing, I tilted my head up to see Kenrick. *Shit!* My mind was no friend of mine at that moment.

I whispered to him, "Please put me down."

"Why? You fit nicely enough."

"I don't belong here and neither do you."

"You are the witch who called me to your side, not I who invaded your secure bed rest."

"I'm not a witch!" I was surprised at him even thinking that of me. I may have visions but I wasn't even close to being pagan, let alone a practicing

Wiccan. I'd been raised as a Methodist, for Christ's sake. Besides, how would he know my religious preferences?

"I politely asked, now I'm demanding. Put me down!"

He grinned down at me. Wasn't he getting tired of holding this cavalier pose? I may be only five-foot-four but I was not a waif. I had curves and strong limbs, even if I'd lost five pounds in the last month. That couldn't be helped as I'd been lean on my grocery shopping budget. I wiggled myself as to make his grip slip but it didn't work. He only chuckled again.

Gritting my teeth, I hissed, "Put. Me. Down."

He did but not exactly how I had hoped. He slid me down his body until I firmly braced myself on my own two feet. And yet I remained against him. Shoving against his solid chest did nothing to bring some personal space between us. It only reminded me he was shirtless in my mental mini-vacation. This needed to stop.

"Fine, if you won't go then state your business and be done with it."

"You still think it's that easy?"

"Yes, Mr. Dream Invader, I do. State your piece and go away. I need my sleep so I can deal with you in reality in the morning."

"How would you deal with me? I'd love to hear this."

"Look, Giles, I'm tired, cranky, out of my element, and scared that I'm going to wake up with a severe anxiety attack if you don't leave me to my meditating."

"We wouldn't want that, now would we?"

"Sexy dreams are great but I'm not in the frame of

mind to deal with this right now."

"I can get you in that wonderful frame of mind. We have a connection, my dear."

"How so?" I asked but he just looked at me, eyes blazing like a cat's caught in firelight.

I gulped as his warmth crept into me. Now I was getting sensations in my head? Next, I'd be doing something embarrassing like having my clothes fall off. Goodness, he was handsome. I squeezed my eyes tight as I fought my subconscious from having that happen. No way. No how. That's when I felt his hand graze down my hair and across my cheekbone. My eyes were wide open with that.

"So soft, like silk and lingerie. Your skin is peaches and cream on a fine china plate. Your eyes are like dusk captured in the reflection of a lake. I can just see the waves of emotion as your expressive face tips up to the light."

Oh good heavens. Poetry was a weakness and he hit me at a low point. But as this was my dream, no wonder he seemed so appealing. I looked into his eyes and it seemed as if a fire burned there. A roaring fire on a cold winter night that captivated me. I felt the heat from those flames and it surprised me. I never got temperature changes or touch during my mental meditations. It was just an exercise to force unwanted things out and leave the quiet of an uncluttered attic. Wide open and peaceful.

This wasn't me. I didn't do this, I'd never even had a wet dream in my whole twenty-six years. I dug my small nails into my fists and fought to disconnect myself from the feel of his skin against mine. I needed to wake up. A stranger was in my dream and he seemed intent on keeping me there. This was my realm. My mind was in charge, not his. I was manifesting this strange dream because I'd been so lonely lately. I'd like to think it was better than one of my stress-induced visions, but those left me drained. This was too intimate for my tired emotions. The need to wake pressed at me.

"Renata?" he whispered as I squeezed my eyes shut so tightly my brow strained.

It wasn't working. "Why can't you just go away?"

"Renata, you are stuck with me, for the time being. I won't apologize as we both have something the other needs."

"Say what?"

"I'll explain this all to you at a later time. You're already overwhelmed and it can wait, as time can be unraveled in the near future. I will make you see. No worries about that, my dear."

I smacked my hands against his chest. It wasn't real after all, so I could do as I pleased. He flinched but didn't release me. I willed him to dissolve into white noise as I felt my head pound with the inner turmoil. That was not a good sign. Then his lips brushed mine and a gasp of shock escaped me.

"How dare you—" My words disappeared as he pressed into me, lips and body.

It was a soft possession but with a hunger which edged on more dangerous things. It felt different than my last few attempts for a good night kiss, especially the one that had me waking on my lumpy den couch, alone.

He spoke against my lips, but I couldn't catch the words. Something sounded vaguely like French. I'd briefly taken a course in high school but it had been many moons ago. Those soft lips grazed against mine again and my breath caught in my tight chest. I formed the word *No* in my mind as if to yell, but he stepped away so quickly I wavered on my feet. As I looked up through my tousled hair, he was gone. Why couldn't he have done that before he kissed me?

****

I woke up with sunlight in my eyes and threw the covers over my sleepy face. I didn't want to wake yet. I'd tossed and turned most of the night and had been up until about two hours ago. No one else had visited in my dream, but I had instantly been caught in a labyrinth impossible to navigate out of. Stretching, I got up to see what was going on in the huge estate. Maybe someone would be able to answer some of my questions while I waited for Mr. White to make an appearance.

I took a quick shower in the adjoining bathroom and decided I would take a leisurely bath in the claw-footed tub if I was too keyed up to sleep tonight. A nap actually sounded great and I never took those. That's just how crappy a night it had been. If there wasn't anyone up for me to speak to then I'd investigate the estate, including the grounds. That led me to pull on my plain hooded sweatshirt with my thick twill khakis. After rubbing some gel into my loose corkscrew curls, I yanked on socks and my old running shoes. I had told myself to forget my makeup bag but something had driven me to put on the basic cosmetics. Maybe I just needed to cover the slight bruising under my troubled eyes? Yes, that was it.

I walked out into the dark wood of the hallway and down the beautifully lacquered winding staircase. Other than a slight trace of dust, the house stood in a wonderful state of care. Almost as if stopped in time but then you would see a few modern conveniences mixed into the vintage décor. It was so comforting that I felt as if I wasn't such an unwelcomed guest. The house felt as warm as the bed I had tossed around in all night.

Seeing the front entrance, I headed that way to walk around the perimeter but the door was pulled open as I pushed upon its heavy weight. I stumbled with a cry but someone caught me before I went halfway down the first stone step. I looked into the familiar eyes of Kenrick. "Oh shit." Then a vision grabbed me faster than the man in front of me.

An ancient, decrepit, and lonely graveyard huddled in the fog of my second sight. Some of the stones were faceless and the statues were of long ago people from a past I wasn't aware of. The heavy air wasn't just the fog of my inner mind but of the bayou on the borders of this property. I pushed toward a stone which had thrummed in the wet ground at my bare toes. I wore a white dress of muslin that brushed the tall grass. The plot had grown up around its inhabitants. So lonely. The marble, which called to me, was so worn from the environment it was no longer a slick cold surface but worn like calloused fingertips. Somehow I knew someone had long ago visited this stone as to touch the person there, missing them with a palpable pain.

The dense air of my vision turned the carved name into a blur my eyes couldn't make out. I traced the letters and brushed against the familiar old rose vine that trailed across the once pure white surface. It was just as decayed as the markers themselves but still held the sharpness of the loss of a loved one. A prick of awareness brought me to the hand laid across those thorns, and the blood sliding down my lace covered wrist. I didn't want the blood on my hands. It was so thick, like it had congealed. So thick. I went to rub it against the rough stone edge but was stopped by a darker hand.

Following the line of the arm up to the face, I looked into topaz eyes that held immense longing. I could feel his pain, like the blood that cooled against my captured hand.

"No. You mustn't," he said softly to me.

I heard voices echo him but no one was with us in that frozen moment. I wish the voices had been people there to take me out of this forgotten place, but the voices had no bodies to claim, not anymore. They felt as old as the land under my feet and as cold as the chill that slipped down my spine.

"The blood can't be on my hands." My reply didn't sound like my usual voice. It was a bit huskier, sexier. Somehow I knew it was me but in a different world. Maybe I had aged by decades in this vision or maybe the voice did belong to someone else. All I knew was it felt like a part of me. There was no explanation for the rest. Most times, I was lucky to even get a clear image that lasted more than a couple of minutes.

"I'll clean the blood away, *cher*. It won't bother you again this day. I promise."

With those words, he gently pulled my hand to his lips and licked a clean line from my fingertips to my beating wrist. Instinct had me wanting to yank my hand back and rub it against the cotton surrounding my fear stricken body. Everything in me screamed to run, yet somehow I couldn't move away from him. I had to get far from this place and never return. Something was wrong here, something beyond my metaphysical knowledge, and I was grateful for the ignorance. I knew then that I couldn't walk away. It was clear to me now.

He continued to cleanse my hand, as I fought not to look at him. He was a cat and I was the bowl of cream which rewarded his deeds of the day. I didn't believe those deeds had been just or good but I wasn't to know what that meant. I peered up at his eyes and they glowed like a bonfire. I screamed and lifted from my nightmare.

Chapter Three

Blinking my heavy eyes open, I took in the concern in his eyes and his creased brows.

"Back up," I lightly grumbled as I reached to push him away but stopped myself. I wasn't anywhere near strong enough to attempt it right now. Touching him had just caused one vision and I wanted to avoid dipping back into that cemetery scene again as the trip had worn me out faster than any other vision before. I'd like to think it was because of the lack of sleep obtained but it was more like it had been a stronger vision than normal for me.

"Are you okay?"

"I'm fine. Just get off of me so I can breathe."

"You are breathing, my dear."

"Stop calling me that, and I won't hyperventilate if you move a safer distance away from me."

He straightened up, and I realized my body was lying across his lap at the front steps. Oh lordy.

Levering myself into a sitting position had me too close to those eyes again. My attempt was less than graceful when I stumbled to my feet, and it took me putting both hands on one of the walls to stop the front door from spinning into the twilight zone. I'd end up with another vision as my nerves felt like living steel drums, which beat a monotonous tune inside my pumping heart. I used my breathing techniques to slow the rate down and then cared to look at the man who had caused all of this.

"Why were you lurking in the doorway?"

"I wasn't. I was simply coming in after watering some of the plants in the yard and caught a woman fainting in the doorway. I do have things to do around here, Miss."

At least he hadn't said my dear again. Another positive was him thinking that was a simple act of fainting instead of my classification as a freak. I didn't know him well enough to tell him the truth, so I let him think me a weak female.

"What do you do around here and where is everyone else?" I used my anger and changed the subject before he asked anything too personal.

"The staff is busy and I do whatever is possible to keep this place up."

"You're making a habit of not fully answering my questions. It seems you either love pulling peoples chains or you are too good to spare the time with a low woman on life's totem pole. Are you looking down your elegant nose at me? Were you lying about Mr. White not telling you about me? Where is he anyway? Have you heard from him at all?"

Kenrick just blinked at me. I was starting to count to ten, if I didn't get any real answers by nine then I'd be in the house by the time I hit ten. He smirked at me by seven and my blood pressure peaked. The hell with eight and nine, I stomped back into the quiet house. Taking my frustration out on something else, I decided to check out the rest of the house and the staff presumably running it. My grandmother had written about a few people in her employment during the renovations she oversaw. Maybe one of them would be amicable. I could only hope.

After thirty minutes of touring on my own, on the main floor, I still hadn't seen anyone else around. Were they all on the second and third floor, maybe outside, or even had the day off? It was Saturday, so their being off could be a safe bet as no one entertained with my step-grandfather passing on. Well, if he had any gatherings after my grandmother had died. She'd told me in her first letter after meeting him that she loved Theodore Fenmore and had positive vibes about the house he'd been refurbishing in hopes she would live with him there. He had told her she was the second wind blowing into his lonely life, and she had said that moment had been very romantic. In hindsight, the only creepy thing I picked up on in her written correspondences was her never mentioning Mr. Giles. I wondered why.

What if he was a squatter and I had spent the night under the same roof with him? Had he been stealing from the house and I'd interrupted his plans to loot the place of everything? I shot back to the main entrance as my mind fleetingly imagined leaving my belongings before heading to some backwoods hotel for the night. I felt like such a total waste of space lately. I had nowhere to go, no money to get there, a sexy stranger as a roommate, and no one to save me within several miles. I was in a stew pot of my own making. These were the times I wished I carried a gun.

I was too close to the last vision to push my luck. I sat on the window seat outside the foyer where I meditated for a few minutes. If Mr. Kenrick Giles showed up, then he could just wait until I was calm enough to deal with his flirty attitude. Being more tired than suspected, I ended up deeper in my safe place than I had thought possible when this keyed up. I shouldn't ever be surprised with my unscrupulous power, no matter how naive I seemed to be. Realizing I had been in here for longer than the intended few minutes, I shook myself back to reality and a less morose frame of mind.

Tummy growling, I headed to the kitchen for a bit of food. There was no telling what there would be to eat if anyone even cooked around this hulk of a house. I walked back to where I'd found the kitchen in the back section of the house, farthest away from the front entrance. No one was there. What the hell? I opened several normal looking doors to see a nice sized pantry of various dried and canned goods, plus one that was not food at all but a walkway so dark it held a heavy oppression.

Cold, stale air wafted over me from the old door. Did it lead downstairs or to a path which took you outside around the house to the barn I'd seen in the distance from one of the kitchen windows? Houses this old could even have hidden passages or service hallways from days long gone. If I ever got to speak to Mr. White, I would add that to my growing list of questions. He may be the only one who could, or would, give me the details needed to see what my future held.

I found the fridge behind another door, and it seemed interesting how they'd made it look like any other door in the room. Was it a way to blend the room into a more seamless look ahead of its time or because the builder liked to throw people for a loop when they came around? It was a bit creepy for my taste as I was used to a simpler lifestyle. I'd hunt Kenrick up for some answers if it would do me any good. He may think I'm insane after my episode earlier. That could be a positive if he was a prowler thinking I was easy prey. If I was crazy then my chances at being left alone were rising to a whole new level. No matter how drawn I was to him, there was no need for him to keep showering me with sexy pick-up lines.

At more complaints from my midsection, I put together a small sandwich from the array of fixings in the fridge doors. I was surprised to see a small assortment of goodies since I wasn't seeing a crew that would be eating them. If they'd had the day off then maybe that was the explanation but a growing ball of nerves was in my stomach at the thought that I truly was alone with an unknown attractive man; a male which kept coming to mind when my eyes were closed. The knot in me had me gulping down the food, with a glass of cold milk, before I took myself back to my room. If I was alone, then I would hope to be safe behind a locked door while I waited for the appearance of Mr. White, if he even bothered to come by. Wait. I'd only seen one phone, and it'd been a cordless by the kitchen pantry. Just another bad sign for my frazzled piece of mind. My basic service cell phone had no connection out here so I wasted my time even turning it on since the dial tone went from high-pitched static to cryptic nothing. Now my bad luck had run from my car to my housemate and into the blasted phone lines. A notepad would be needed if the list of things to question got much larger.

Cleaning up my small mess, I headed to investigate more of the house as I impatiently waited for Mr. White to show himself. If I was lucky, I'd be able to skip seeing my unfortunate housemate. A part of me hoped he would be gone for the rest of the day, especially after I freaked out in front of him, but the other part of me was curious about him and his good looks. He wasn't my typical type, but then again, what was typical about me? Thinking it over, ticking off the pros and cons, I understood the chemistry in his eyes. They held something that speared right into me. His shoulders were nice and surprisingly broad for such a slender waist and he had long legs with graceful lean hands. Full lips and tousled hair the color of chocolate dipped in caramel were tied for second on my list of favorites on this male menu. But his mesmerizing gaze of amber laced with mischief intent entranced me.

Since this was the wrong topic to be thinking on, I forced myself to keep walking the halls. The door in front of me seemed to have cool air seeping from it, like the door in the kitchen. Silence surrounded me so I knew no one was in that quiet room. It gave me the courage to slip the door open and see if I was correct about a breeze from an open window. Wow. Not only was I right but I was in a library worthy enough to make any book lover weep. The scents of leather and old paper rode the air coming in the fully open window by the mahogany desk. Beside a vintage picture of a rose garden, I saw a high-backed chair in a warm gold hue. Grabbing up a leather-bound volume of poems, I sat in the chair and decided to occupy my time while I pondered topics for my expected guest. *If* the lawyer was going to show.

After reading a few, the pages blurred. I rubbed at my eyes but I still fell into a half-dream state of languor. A knock came to the door but I didn't feel like opening my eyes so they would gaze upon a man who would only annoy me, so I let sleep claim me. In my subconscious, I thought out all the ways an encounter could turn out if I had been awake. Or he could have thought I was ignoring him, as he deserved that much after his flirtations last night. I joyfully dreamed his pride was injured by my refusal to quit the pretense at catnapping. The version that played had him striding up to me anyway, the arrogant bastard. I fought to keep my eyes from flickering around under my closed lids as his warm breath caressed my nose. If I was lucky, then he'd take my guise for truth and leave me to my peace. The only man I wanted a conversation with was the elusive attorney.

I felt the brush of fingertips at the wispy bangs that tickled across my skin with his deep exhalation. It's like he breathed a sigh of relief that I was unaware of his presence. As if. I couldn't stop my nose from wrinkling as he ran a feather-light skim across it. Damn, I was betraying my act. Quickly, I acted as if I swatted away an annoying fly, close to the truth, and kept my eyes closed as I readjusted in my chair. I had slumped enough the hood of my sweatshirt wadded behind my neck and would be bound to cause a cramp if I had to carry this act much longer. I was enjoying my little acting bit as a way to put a dent in his narcissistic armor. But he wasn't leaving. In fact, I heard him move a piece of furniture in front of my still figure. What the hell was he up to?

His shadow fell over me, as the light was more firmly blocked away from my hooded vision. My body tightened, tense enough now to flinch if he touched me again. My heart thudded a harsh beat as I fought my mind to calm my fleeing courage. And I did jump. Something light pressed against my limp mouth and as I betrayed myself, so did my mind. The pressure got heavier and heavier as he made his presence known. The idiot was kissing me. My eyes flew open as I acted as if he woke me from my nap.

Sitting up quickly, he took advantage of the situation and claimed my shoulders in his lean hands. I blinked up at him as if I was a deer waiting to be hit by the karma bus. It wouldn't have gone this far if I had banished the act and told him to go the fuck away. I mumbled against his lips but the compression of his kiss didn't allow me to do anything but get a small gasp out. That was all he needed. He tugged me closer to his body as he sat on the footstool I had glimpsed by the loveseat. I was moved so quickly I had to stabilize myself before I possibly fell off the edge of the chair.

My hands were on his knees and his arms stole around my upper body as it unintentionally slid forward. A grunt came from me and his kiss became more than pressure, more than a chaste stealing of the moment. His legs opened, pulling my braced body closer to his. In a rapid move, I placed my palms against his chest and had every intention of pushing this cretin away from me. How was it possible for him to think this was going to be allowed? Was he insane?

Maybe I was the one who had lost their mind because instead of pushing him away I fisted my hands in his cotton shirt. He needed to be off of me. So why wasn't I stopping him? I was actually taking part in the kiss. If you count my lips joined with his as an acting part of this madness. A cold breeze arrowed in through the open window and seemed to push between us. A cold flick of a windy hand as if to deter us. I shivered. A soft growl came from the man in front of me and it shocked a gasp out of me. That's what tipped the balance to his side as he took my open mouth in an exploring kiss.

He treated me like a first taste of some new exotic dish on a delicate gold-rimmed plate. His tongue delved in and took his time as he tasted me. It was how I approached a fine piece of dark chocolate. He savored the sensation as he melted against me. His tongue rasped against mine as I sat stock still in his arms. I lost it as he slipped a hand into my hair and massaged my scalp. I'd always loved having someone play with my hair but had never had it done like this, in a kiss. I met his kiss and his hunger seemed to go up a notch. He was devouring this piece of chocolate and may well be on his way to finishing it off.

Another breeze came through the room and wrapped around us like a cold and clammy hand. It bathed me in a coldness which brought me back to my senses. I jolted away from him as if the wind had smacked me back to the chair. His desire filled eyes looked at me in utter surprise as his stool suddenly pushed away from me in a wild gust. What the hell? The wind whipped back to me as it slapped against my flushed face. Then my book hit the floor with a thump which woke me up.

Jumping so hard, I almost fell out of the chair. When I looked around my book was indeed on the floor, but how had I incorporated it into my dream? The window was still open but the drapes were in total disarray, as if the wind had been as real as the book which had fallen from my startled body. Was I losing my mind or was the house just bringing out my fears? I had to shake it off and not let these little things throw me into a tailspin. That had happened once and I wasn't about to be hospitalized again. Not like before. Not ever again.

I picked up the book and shelved it back in its home on the floor to ceiling bookshelf. There were so many books I could live here for years and not run out of things to read. I even glimpsed a few of the occult and witchcraft among the well-read classics. Here there was no dust to cover the rich leathers of the old bindings. It was as if they had been saved from a life of abuse. If only we could all be protected like this. It made me ache but I shoved it away, as usual, to go about a life that I had to fix. I seemed to be the kind of person who walked around being covered in invisible bandages, waiting to be healed. One day, I would be. I had vowed to myself on the day I had been admitted for being a hazard to myself. I had to carry that burden on my own two thin shoulders.

Silently clicking the door closed on the strange moment in the library, I moved on to another part of the house. This and the books were the only things I could do to occupy my time as I waited for the next step in my disheveled life. I found my way out the back terrace doors of the main living room to find a greenhouse in the distance. It was the old-fashioned type with warped green glass and rusty metal girders. Breathtaking in its solemn state, I was drawn forward.

It had a neglected stone walkway which had seen better days but you could see the details of the swirls drawn into the cement as it had dried. The larger picture showed a vine carrying you into the open doorway of the building. How charming? Even if slightly neglected, the greenhouse was still in use as there were tomatoes, flowers, and herbs in the boxes in rows by the tall green-tinted walls. The herbs were carefully labeled and the flowers ranged from a few orchids to a small leafed poinsettia. Where the library had been chilling yet welcoming, this was an unsettling warm embrace against my jagged nerves. Shivering, I pushed away the image of a demon breathing its molten fire at me.

It was growing dark as I finished my tour of the greenery around me. Suddenly, a beam of headlights floated down the front wall of the greenhouse. A car was creeping up the graveled driveway of the estate. Dusting off my hands, I made my way up to the end of the driveway so I could get a better view of who was gracing us with an appearance. I calmly waited as I rubbed a new chill from my limbs and hoped it was the attorney bringing me good news. If the temperatures persisted then I may need heavier clothes, if my meager budget allowed. My case only had about two dozen pieces in it, which were mix and match items streaming from business casual to just plain slouchy. I might have to bundle up in layers of the more summer attire or just place a throw around my shoulders like a wrap, for moments like this one. I normally wasn't so sensitive to cold but this place could seep into my bones. My thinking had me wondering if I was moving from ghostly cold spots into monster riddled staleness while trekking from place to place in the estate. I couldn't put into words the eerie sensations that prickled across my skin in some of the areas I had stood in.

The 1972 white luxury sedan came up like a still

from a classic movie but there was no femme fatale in the back of the four-door vehicle. Once stopped, out stepped a very thin man wearing a somber gray suit which matched his worn leather briefcase. His hair was a few wisps of steel gray waving in a sudden breeze from the direction of the driveway. He wore simple horn-rimmed glasses over beady eyes surrounded by fine wrinkles. If he were a dog then he'd be an anorexic dark sharpei. His bearing carried sad tidings better than the suit that swarmed his frame.

"You must be Ms. Renata. I'm Mr. Thorton White of White and Company Attorneys. I hope your travel here was a gentle one," he stated in a weak voice as he offered me a bony hand.

I paused at his phrasing but took his hand to receive a limp handshake.

"Yes, and I've been wondering when you would arrive."

"My apologies, ma'am. I'm one of the few attorneys in town so times can get very tense when disparity falls around the district."

"Well, I hope everything is going to be okay."

He gave me a deep look. "So do I. Now, let's go into the house so we can cover the legalities which bring us together. Shall we?"

He motioned me forward and I began the walk back into the darkened house. As I'd been outside and not used to the lack of lights, I hadn't thought about the house being layered in shadows. It wasn't my house and it just slipped my mind, which was not my normal attention to detail. Mr. White walked to a side table and retrieved a small box of matches in a manner that had me realizing just how well he knew the insides of this place. Striking one, he walked to the brass candle holder by the staircase and lit the slim cream taper. I may have to carry a flashlight around with me while I'm here, if I could find one.

"You have already realized your grandfather might have liked his modern conveniences but he abhorred fake lighting. That's why there are so many windows but no lamps around the estate. He saw no need in installing humming fluorescent bulbs to guide him to bed at night."

"I find it odd as there are other ways of solving the problem," I stated out loud and then saw a semblance of a wry smile cross the old man's face.

"Yes, we have many a southern eccentric out here but you get used to their ways after a while. If you choose to stay then you can make any changes you see fit within the confines of the will."

I squeaked as out of the dark, behind me, a smooth voice invaded the conversation. "Sir, will you be needing me this evening?"

"Mr. Giles, good evening." They shook hands like old friends. "Yes, I will need to discuss a few things with you but not until after my talk with the young Ms. Renata. What room would be best to use as we discuss the sad matters at hand?"

I was still getting my heart to slow down as I turned to see the shape of Kenrick in the shadows behind me. He stepped forward, to the edge of the flame lit area, and a side of his face was brought into view. That handsome face looked straight at me. "The lady's library will suit you well."

Chapter Four

The lack of light hid my blush as I glanced at the chair I had vacated hours ago. Kenrick had led us up here without the use of any light so he had to have been around here for a long measure of time if he had the entire layout memorized like this. I had thought he had done this simply to mess with me but he had a gift for this creepy meandering in the void of lights. He had been kind enough to have lit another candle off of Mr. White's as we had all gotten into the room, for my benefit. Mr. White had been left with the other candle as he had claimed that old men needed more light than the younger generation. The window was now closed and Kenrick placed the brass holder on the desk in front of the array of glorious bookcases.

Why this room when there were plenty of other rooms ready for company? I would have been just as comfortable in the main living area than up here where I'd had that intimate dream. And why had Kenrick looked at me when he'd mentioned coming up here. It's not like he would have known he was the star in that unconscious moment. I averted my face as Kenrick looked at us before leaving us in private. Was I reading too much into his piercing gaze? Lord. My face was flaming.

As soon as the door had clicked shut, Mr. White set his candle on the desk, opened his leather case, and pulled a stack of paperwork from the worn depths. I chose to sit on the floral print loveseat instead of the chair from before. I just couldn't get over my embarrassment at what my mind had pictured when I had been so drained from my vision. Maybe it was the supernatural sexiness of the vision that had brought my sleeping self into a kiss from the lips which had licked blood from my skin. I was getting a headache from all of this, not to mention slightly turned on at the feeling of his lips on my skin, reality or not.

"Ms. Renata, as you know, your step-grandfather passed away in his sleep over three weeks ago after succumbing to several illnesses. He had been fading away since your grandmother had left him last year. I would venture to say he was dying of a broken heart once she had crossed over without him."

"I know the autopsy had said she had died of natural causes but I still believe there is more to it than that. If I hadn't been told I could lose my job, then I would have been here to question things at the funeral. Now, no one is around to answer my inquiries about the whole matter."

He had opened the topic so I sucked down the tears to use this to my advantage.

"Yes, I can see how you would think that as she was found by the cemetery the day of her passing, God rest her soul. But there were no wounds or signs of foul play at the site. It was pronounced a heart attack, and I have satisfied myself with that conclusion."

"Didn't anyone think it strange for a woman of good health to be found like that by the cemetery? Why was she out there, and why didn't her doctor see she was physically sliding downhill?"

"Madam, I'm not knowledgeable about her health, as my specialty was not involved. Your family never let on any concerns where their health lay so I left it to them to handle. I'm only the attorney, not their physician, so I can only apologize for your loss. I was proud to know those wonderful people."

Keeping fresh tears from leaking down my face, I was aware of how rude I was being to a man just as in the middle of this as I was.

"That being water under the bridge, what do we need to handle as of this moment? He was cremated and had his ashes mixed with the soil on my grandmother's grave, so no further arrangements are needed."

"Ms. Renata, I am aware of your frustration at the situation but you had mentioned on the phone that you had not been able to visit with your family after the recent circumstances since college. Neither of us is to blame for the sad happenings since then but we will both do what is needed to get through the next few stages."

Being properly chastised by an elder, I stomped my hurt feelings aside. "I apologize for my negative way of approaching this but you must realize I'm confused and displeased with the lack of information given to me the last year."

"You must also be feeling guilty for not having the time to spare for them since you left the campus to pursue your career, but these things do happen for adults who are spreading their wings. At my last visit with her she had stated how wonderful it had been to visit you at your dorm, so know that she was very proud of you."

"She was the best family I could have asked for

and my regret is a weight I will have to bear."

After a moment of awkward silence, he cleared his throat and began shuffling through the papers at his fingertips.

"I'm afraid to say you will not be comfortable with the decision in front of you. There are two options stipulated in the will and as you are the remaining member of your grandmother's family, a majority of the estate has been left to you."

Shock was an understatement.

"Did he not have any family at all?"

"You might find it strange but he never had any children before he met your grandmother and she had given birth to your father many years before she had met your step-grandfather. The whole of the estate is the house and its sixteen acres of property, which include the pecan orchard, the cemetery, the greenhouse, and 2.5 million dollars."

Holy shit.

He continued, "The house and all its trappings, the investment of his family money, plus the contracts with the neighbors, equal a total net worth of approximately 4.5 million dollars."

Breath halted. Time stopped. My heart bounded.

"Excuse me?" I squawked.

He actually smiled for all of a second and then washed it away with his more customary mood of sad tidings. "It is a shocking amount but Mr. Fenmore was from old money that had been invested in oil before his marriage to your grandmother. A sum of the money had been used to update the plantation once Mrs. Kenmore decided to move in. He had her complete any changes she wished as long as the lighting and a few other areas were left as they were," he added with a ghost of a smirk.

"That would explain why she didn't install lamps around the house. I still find it unusual but I'm not one to throw stones on that regard. Please, go on."

"Having the house stay in this state is still part of the guidelines but normal updating is acceptable. I have been instructed that my office will be holding the escrow account for the upkeep of the estate in its entirety. We have a detailed list of what is approved for any changes and a list just as long of what is not."

Figures.

"Here is where we get deeper into the situation. Mr. Fenmore still has business dealings and they will be carried into the future by the shareholders of the oil company he founded. The interest from that will be deposited into the account, as usual. Mr. Giles will be offered a chance to stay on and look over the maintenance of the estate, as he has been for the last few years."

"So that's what he does around here?"

"He would be named as the caretaker, if you had to put a title to the duties he performed for your family. Your grandmother agreed to him being hired after she moved in and began treating him like a son."

"He's barely said anything to me about this so it's comforting to know where he stands in this. What else can you tell me?"

"I know little about Mr. Giles other than what has been shared with me. You are normal in wondering about the man but anything you need further answers on will have to be asked of him. I don't like third tales in anything other than facts entailed in the case itself."

"I respect that."

"Good. I can give you a list of the smaller details of the will, if you agree to stay at the estate for another few days. Mr. Fenmore wanted you to get a feel for the property as you pondered over the paperwork. He thought it was fair so you could make a more precise decision about your future."

"Anything I need to know about while I'm taking the time to follow your instruction?"

"Normal activity will resume here as you get your bearings. In two days' time, I will be back to hear what you have chosen to do. I've already scheduled the next pick up of pecans and you will have Mr. Giles here to see to any details needing to be handled as you absorb your surroundings."

"What about the rest of the crew? Does that mean they will be staying on with whichever person owns the property?"

He quirked a thin eyebrow at me. "What crew would that be, Ms. Renata?"

"Aren't there more employees working here? A chef, a gardener, or a maid? Somebody?"

"No, it's just you and our Mr. Giles."

"Excuse me?" I said, in a state of mild shock.

"As Mr. Fenmore got more depressed, he let more of his staff go. He had not felt that he needed very many people watching over the place after your grandmother had been taken away. You weren't aware of this?"

"I was not informed and I wonder what else has been neglected in that same category."

"Pardon me, as I had presumed you and Mr. Giles would have a discussion about the current standings of things. I will speak with Mr. Giles and see what needs to be gone over."

"Thank you and your help is appreciated in these legal matters."

"My apologies for any inconvenience and I will see what can be done for you. I'll give you this list of paperwork to browse over and will gather up Mr. Giles. Excuse me."

He handed me a thick clip of folders before leaving the room in search of the elusive Mr. Giles. I would have gladly walked away from the room for them to talk but why should I be the one to tuck tail when I hadn't done anything wrong? I was being overly sensitive, but I'd had enough of this cryptic attitude toward my future. I went to the vast list of items my step-grandfather left to me. That's when the breath escaped me like a kick to the midsection.

The total monthly income from interest alone added up to more than three months of my old income. I was giddy until I reminded myself this wasn't my money and there were strings to deal with if I became a puppet of the estate. I needed to be aware of every semblance of fine print in order to make the best decision for myself on this new land in front of me. Included was the utilities and general upkeep of the estate, which had to be headed by Kenrick or by the attorney trust. There was no housekeeper or gardener, as Mr. White had mentioned, but I could hire them from the yearly budget set aside for anything needed on the estate as a whole. Would I want to use some funds for people in here or would I try to keep up the duties myself? It was something to check into.

The cemetery and greenhouse were to be kept up,

with the grounds around them not getting into any undesirable state. I hadn't even been back there to see if there were weeds taking over the faded tombstones. I'd have to make a trip out there tomorrow to see what was needed with landscaping. But I sure wasn't going to tromp around right now, not at half-past creep thirty.

My eyes bulged at what was written in the next clause. Mr. Kenrick Giles was welcome to live on the property, as he currently was, for as long as he desired and there had been no limitations put upon him. What the hell? And neither of us were allowed to sell the place while we were alive. It had to be handed down to someone worthy of the estate for it to change hands at all. I wasn't getting a wonderful property; I was getting to be a babysitter for a grown man who had somehow squeezed himself into the stubborn crevices of my stepgrandfather's heart. Not to mention my dried-out libido. How had he weaseled in with my grandmother? Simple, she had a kind heart and always voted for the underdog, which had been me since I was small. Now they had set me up to live with a complete and utter stranger who had me thinking of husky whispers in silken sheets.

"This is fucking insane!"

"Pardon me?" asked Kenrick from behind me.

I jumped. I was going to have to put a bell on the man.

"Is everything all right, Ms. Renata?" asked Mr. White.

"Sure. I was just surprised over some of the fine print in the paperwork," came from between my clenched teeth. They probably thought the worst of me after waltzing in on my outburst.

"Do you have any questions for me or do you need some time to digest this?"

"Time is needed for my decision, but I have questions. Do you have time to answer a few of them before you go?

"Yes, Ms. Renata, I can spare a few moments, but I must be leaving soon."

"Why the urgency? Do you have another appointment this evening?"

"No, ma'am, you were my last one for the day."

Something about his answers raised warning flags in me.

"I know you're on retainer and can bill the estate for your time, so why do I get the feeling you'd like to be out of here as quickly as possible?"

It was the nicest way I could ask without being rude again. I had even forced a small smile with my words so it was taken in a warmer light.

"It's simply my distaste for driving in the dark of night. Nothing more."

My mind was telling me there was more to it but I didn't know this man well enough to interrogate him about his everyday practices.

Kenrick spoke up from the doorway. "I will leave the two of you to your discussion while I go check on a couple of things."

"No, Mr. Giles. You can stay as you are a part of this particular conversation. I hate backstabbing so you can hear what I have to say, unless you'd rather hear all of this secondhand, as I have been treated the last day or so," I stated my point as nicely as possible.

"I'll be right over here as you ask your questions," Kenrick replied as he stalked to the window and gave us his back.

He had countered with a snide remark of his own by turning his back to us. Fine. I saw that as a point for myself and not for the quiet man who was treating me like an outcast in a home which could very well be mine. I actually saw the cogs spinning in the attorney's lined face as he confirmed my suspicions with his next set of words.

"If I'm going to be questioned about the relationship between Mr. Giles and the late Mr. Fenmore then that is confidential and up to Mr. Giles to share if he so chooses. I can only answer the questions relevant to the legalities of the situation."

"This is about the legalities and what brought them on."

"Ms. Renata, please be assured I will do what I can but some things are not meant for me to discuss."

I'd reword it then. "What transpired for my step-grandfather to make sure Mr. Giles was included in the will? You two are acting like co-conspirators and I'm needing to make sure all of this truly is on the up and up."

"Again, ma'am, I can speak only of my professional dealings and not on a personal level," Mr. White said as he stared at his folded hands.

"Can't or won't?" I asked.

"Both. I must not so I cannot. My apologies but I have sworn some things to secrecy and must uphold my honor, even if it leads you to think ill of me."

"Mr. White, it's not just you that I question. With what has been shown me so far, I'm wondering if it's more drama than it's worth. I should just say goodbye to all of this and simply walk away."

"But you can't. Can you?" interrupted Kenrick from his quiet corner.

We both turned our heads to the man who had spoken.

"Yes, I can go anytime I want to," I retorted.

"Where would you go?" he asked quietly.

"That's my business, isn't it?"

"Then why is my reason for being here any of yours?"

"A bit of that may be true but your being here affects my decision and my life."

"Just as your decision will affect what will happen to me."

Touché, even if I didn't like it.

"Mr. Giles makes a valid point. As of our last phone conversation, you had lost your job and were on the same path with your housing as no money would be coming your way. Did something change that I'm not aware of?" asked Mr. White.

"Um, no. But it is my problem to solve."

"Yes, it is but what's being handed to you will affect more than one person."

"How so?"

"If you leave now, then the money is forfeit, as is the entirety of the estate. The proceeds will all be turned over to Mr. Kenrick Giles as the sole inheritor. You walk away with what you came with, nothing."

Chapter Five

"That was rude and uncalled for!" I stated in disgust.

"My apologies but this was getting off topic from what needs to be discussed at this time." Mr. White nervously looked at his watch, again.

"Are you sure you don't have plans for this evening?" I questioned.

"No, Ms. Renata, but I do need to be going soon."

I had the sense he was looking for any reason to get out of here, quickly. What was going on that had him losing his professional attitude?

Then I heard thunder rumble in the distance, beyond the window in front of Kenrick. He still had his back to us and I couldn't see his reflection for the froth of curtains that covered a portion of the framed glass. Why did I suddenly need to see his eyes? No clue.

"Mr. White, do I have this correct that I am to accept the terms of the will as they stand or leave and forfeit all rights to anything in the estate, even my grandmother's things?"

"You understand correctly."

I saw Mr. White look over his left shoulder to where Kenrick stood quietly. Was he waiting on a sign from him before giving anything away? Seriously? And why was Kenrick so calmly stoic in the middle of me questioning his presence here? I would have been offended. Maybe he knew I wanted him to spill some kind of information. If he did then he knew this game well.

"Fine, I want the time to read over things, which means I agree to stay overnight and will meet the stipulation of being paid the five thousand dollars, correct? Does that mean that I can actually have a key to this place or will that have to wait until I say whether I'll agree to the terms of the will as a whole?"

"Yes, Ms. Renata. The key would come once the terms are settled. If you chose to walk away after staying for forty-eight hours, then you get the money mentioned to you and nothing more. You will leave this place to Mr. Giles and the estate will go on as it did before you arrived," he said it with a sudden flick of nervous eyes at Kenrick.

"If everything is agreeable for the night, then may I walk you out, Mr. White?"

"Yes, please," Mr. White said as he quickly grabbed up his briefcase of papers and began to leave the room.

"What is the hurry, gentlemen?"

"If you must know, Mr. White dislikes storms. Do you, sir?" Kenrick asked the man heading to the door of the library.

Mr. White barely turned to face me as he walked over the threshold and into the hallway. "No, Mr. Giles. I do not and it's slightly embarrassing to admit it. Good night, Ms. Renata."

Then I was left in the room, alone. So I had made him admit something scared him? We all hid something away from the face of fear and this house seemed to yank it out of all of us.

I reread the passage about Kenrick Giles being part of the estate as if he was a fixture of the building. I knew there was something not being told to me but they weren't in a sharing mood. I'd just have to stay here and try to figure things out. Did I want to be here and make this estate my new home or run away with my stipend and find a hovel to rebuild myself? It was too much information for me to take. If I took the estate then I would have to deal with Mr. Kenrick Giles on a never-ending basis. Could I find a peaceful compromise between the two of us? I couldn't answer that right now. What parts of this could I break down tonight?

There were a few options open to me. Do the things I'd only dreamed of by staying and accepting the offer with a blind eye to the nagging little ideas in my head. See if something had happened for my family to have accepted Kenrick into the household, like a dark tragedy. Three, the longer that Mr. White had been here, the jumpier he had gotten, and I knew something was behind it. Was he scared of the house, to be around Kenrick, or could it be as simple as an older man's phobia? Four, no, I didn't have anywhere to go. That in itself was a touchy subject for me. I had been independent for years but now I had to live off of people who were practically strangers to me.

Having already received my severance letter with my last check, I was filled with possibilities and anxiety over the chance to recreate my life in the last home my grandmother had lived in.

Fighting the tears that burned in my eyes, I rebuked myself again for life issues keeping me away from the one person who had accepted me for what I was—a troubled woman who feared the prolonged touch of anything. I was thrown into visions that took over during any emotional weakness or moments of exhaustion. I had been in the presence of my grandmother when I'd had one that had knocked me out cold, and she had held me as I'd seen the inner story of her losing my biological grandfather. Experiencing it had been rough on both of us, but she had helped me come to terms with my curse and taught me the first lessons on how to keep it at bay. Without that honest southern dame, I would have stayed in the psychiatric ward where my parents had temporarily put me after they had overheard me telling my grandmother about a particular troubling vision I experienced while at school. That had been the worst two weeks of my existence, and now I was facing a life where no one would, or could, love me as the freak I was.

Then a realization slammed into me, I hadn't gotten Mr. White's cell phone number. Tossing down the stack of papers and running for the front stairs, I heard no voices. Maybe they were out by his car. I ran through the front door like the lightning that struck in the clouds above me. Fast and with a heart-thumping purpose. The car was gone. How had he gotten out of here so quickly? I hadn't even heard his old sedan turn down the gravel drive. Then I glimpsed the taillights as they blinked at me through the dense set of trees which flanked the driveway. He was already turning onto the main road, leaving me with no way to communicate with him this weekend. I'd have to ask Kenrick for the attorney's cell phone number but I doubted he'd be so generous after I questioned his presence at the estate.

I traipsed back in with a pout as it dawned on me how ridiculous this all was. A majority of this was my fault, but it would be easier for me to swallow if I could take it out on someone else, childish or not. It would be karma for me to have to serve humble pie tomorrow afternoon.

I dove into the house when a voice came from the dark behind me.

"If you were looking to stop him, it's too late."

Mentally, I just added large bells onto the collar needed on his strong neck, before I strangled it. What humble pie?

"I simply wanted his cell phone number so I could contact him with any further questions I might have over the next twenty-four hours."

"Like what else you can get from staying here or maybe you wanted to sneak a peek at personal items that are none of your business?"

"I'm not the money hound here, sir," I said as indignantly as possible.

"So, you think I did something dastardly to be here. Is my assumption correct?"

"What else am I to think when you won't state how you came to be here in the first place? You had to have done something remarkable to be the next heir to all of this when you were only in the picture the past couple of years."

"*If* you walk away, remember?"

"Either way, you stand to gain from this whereas I'm not so lucky."

"You can take the money offered for the forty-eight-hour marker and run away to start another life for yourself. Take it while you have the chance. The only thing here for you is an estate of ageless pain and stale blood. What would a beautiful woman want with it?"

Was I more stunned by his use of words or the compliment he'd just issued with the cryptic comment?

"What is so terrible that neither of you will talk about it? I already know both Fenmores died on the property so it's not that. It's something about how you came to be here and I know it's a detail that will affect my life if I stay on. I can't explain it but I have to be told the truth." I was gesturing in the air as if conjuring the right words by magic.

"An estate of this age has more than one secret."

"And apparently, so do the people involved with it. Look, if you aren't going to help me then just go away and leave me alone."

"I did help you. I just told you to take the money and run. That's all that needs to be said. Unless you're looking for action, which I can provide in spades."

Floundering with the endless comebacks, I just stared at him like a dead fish. And with that, he turned his back on me and headed toward the rear of the grounds with his hands stuffed in his pants pockets.

He had to have serious mental problems. Coming from me, that was saying something. Was he some dude hiding from the law or possibly post-traumatic stress syndrome I was witnessing? Was this his refuge from society? Did he want me gone badly enough to try scaring me away from all of this? Were the pick-up lines meant to make me feel uncomfortable having him around? Couldn't my life be simple? All I've ever wanted was a place of my own and enough money to stay out of debt permanently. There were no plans for a fancy new car, a whole different wardrobe, or a man who would pamper me from head to toe. I was just looking for a satisfyingly simple life that kept me from the fears which had already put me in a singular spotlight of despair.

I saw the small candlestick Mr. White had taken down with him as he'd made his hasty departure and thankfully it was still lit. It had melted down to half of what it had been when we had started the visit, which made me feel even more confused at how quickly scenarios kept turning. Carefully picking up the candle, I made my way back to the second-floor library where the papers were waiting for me. As I placed the glowing stick on the desk, I felt the breeze from the half-opened window. When had it been opened? Kenrick must have come up a back way and opened it just to freak me out. I went to close it but the soft rumbling outside was a strange comfort, so I left it as it was. If it started raining onto the fluffy rug, then I'd close it for the night.

My candle was still by the chair, as I'd left it there in my haste to run to the door. If it hadn't been for the one left downstairs then I probably would've missed a step and hurt myself. I hadn't even thought about it until seated safely back upstairs. People did uncharacteristic things when driven by adrenaline.

I read over the papers again, this time reading all of the legal items that were only to be translated by the attorney who had run out of here. I grabbed a pen and a scratch pad out of the top middle desk drawer to make a list of things to ask the attorney. I was tempted to write *"who is Mr. Kenrick?"* on every other line but stopped myself. He already knew I wanted an answer along that line and I despised how drawn I was to a man who could mean nothing but trouble for me.

When I started the second page of questions, lightning spread through the room and took the last of the light with it as it left in a stiff wind. I was in a darkness that was touchable. I sat for a panic-stricken moment as my eyes adjusted to the instant lack of light. I got a moment of sight when lightning struck again but it only messed further with my eyes. I needed a flashlight or a covered hurricane lamp if this was how the rest of my night would be going. If my step-grandfather had hated ceiling lights then why hadn't he used better ways of lighting the place? Everyone I knew had a range of emergency lights around their houses. This would be my first order of business, that is if I chose to move in. Every room would have a secondary set of lights, if I couldn't install anything into the ceilings then there would at least be a flashlight housed in each room. Maybe it was just the type of lighting he despised and not the need for them alone. It was insane. Leave it to my fabulous grandmother to have married into a family more eccentric than the one she had in me.

Not being able to sit as the darkness wrapped around me, I fumbled my way to the mantel by the door to the hallway. I recalled the matches being left there when we'd come into the room, so they must be there for me to put flame to the remainder of the candles. After stubbing my toes on what felt like a chair, I got the matchbook and scratched one to life so I could make it to the desk without further damage.

It went out after a gust blew into the room and snuffed out my first attempt. I moved quickly to set it ablaze again and this time I succeeded. I cupped my hand over the small flame and prayed it wouldn't go out again. There were only two matches left and I had no clue as to where the others were kept, or new candles, for that matter. I had left a candle in my room from last night, so that was something. I would leave the smaller of the two used candles in here for later, if I couldn't find any more before going to bed.

I could have just made my way to my room and stayed there all night but I was too keyed up to just fall into bed. I was just plain annoyed. Using my pent-up angst, I made my way slowly to the kitchen where I fixed myself a peanut butter and honey sandwich. This comfort food would be even better with a few cups of tea. Putting down my food, I looked through the pantry for the tea I had glimpsed earlier. There was a peppermint green tea which would suit my mood and I went to fill the tea kettle hanging by the stove hood. I got a flame out of the fancy gas range and set to making my tea.

I retrieved my sandwich and sat down at the breakfast table to wait for the water to warm up. Halfway done with my dinner, I heard a scream which pierced my temples.

"I see you found the murderous tea kettle."

I squealed, like the little girl that I was.

Kenrick yanked the screeching kettle off of the burner before my yelp finished echoing against the walls of the kitchen. My heart thudded so hard it was a lump I had to swallow around. He set the offending metal on an opposite burner after filling up a cup from a rack on the other side of the stove. Bringing the steaming cup to me, he took the other head of the table. I went about making my cup of tea, using the honey I had left out after making my sandwich. He just quietly stared at me while I went through the motions of something that should have been soothing. He'd turned it into something else.

"Can I help you?" I questioned as I palmed my near sweltering cup.

My tone was hotter than the liquid my breath was blowing on.

"No, no one can do that. I'm here to see if I can be of assistance to you before I retire for the evening."

"Now you want to be helpful?" I laughed, then sipped at the cooled surface of my drink.

He just kept looking at me like he was waiting for more than just a random set of questions.

"What is your deal?" I asked as I put down the china.

"I'm a complicated man with a sad history. A gentleman was kind to me, so I stuck around and helped where I could."

"It sounds too simple for the enigma we're in together."

"That's my background on being here in simple terminology."

"How come you didn't tell me all along that we were the only two people in this massive place?"

"You didn't ask."

"Why do you keep disappearing?"

"You saw me handle things around the place, so that question was already answered."

"Ugh, you are such a pain in the ass!"

"That isn't a question," he said quietly as he got up from his chair.

"What? You're going to walk away after three questions? Are you some enchanted genie here to annoy the piss out of me?"

He shook his head and walked away. I smacked my hand against the tabletop in frustration. I wanted to snatch him up and make him answer me but it would only get me prisoned for assault and battery. He wasn't worth jail time. I poured another cup of tea and forced myself to calm down. I so didn't need the stress of this. If he was in constant asshole mode then I didn't need him as a roommate either. The thought of him doing this to make me want to leave was quickly becoming more realistic in my mind. He'd have the place to himself for the rest of his life. And I certainly didn't see this man having a child to hand it all over to. So, what his reason for staying? Just one more thing that made me think my handsome estate mate was indeed a money hound. A hound with a very kissable mouth, sadly.

I finished my cup and washed it out as I cleaned up before I retired to bed. I had had enough of today and just wanted it to be over before I stressed myself into another vision. Would it always be this way here? I certainly hoped not because I'd be back at the asylum, booking a suite for an undetermined amount of time. I said an old prayer of peace and light as I walked upstairs and made my shadowy way to my closed bedroom door.

I scrubbed my face in the quaint bathroom and slipped into my comfortable pajama set that wasn't worn for its looks. They were a faded pair of men's small cotton pajamas which were once a proud red but had succumbed to a washed out pink. Even if they were threadbare in a few places, they carried the warmth I needed tonight. As the storm was rolling into the quiet house, my chills rose to meet the strange electricity in the air.

My visionary issues were bad enough without an extra ounce of power in the atmosphere. Some storms were like a static-covered blanket being wrapped around my sensitive frame. It could be a layer of warmth but it could also be uncomfortable, like clothes two sizes too small. Tonight, was closer to the latter with my nerves being on edge from the happenings of the day. Was it too much to ask for the simple life again? Would it be possible with the acceptance of the estate? Somehow, I doubted it was my staying here for a couple of nights that had me on a binge of emotions that gathered too easily in the pit of my stomach.

Sitting on the bed, Indian style, had me where I could nudge myself into a more suitable space to meditate. Using the rumble from the sky as my white noise, I focused my mental hands to push aside the house and all 16 acres, the papers that waited for me in the library, the attorney with his strange way of dealing with me, the vision from earlier, and just as I went to give the greatest shove of them all to Kenrick Giles, two things happened. First, the candle on the nightstand blew out in a single puff of sound and he grabbed me back. As I had to be in a dream state for him to be with me, time must have slunk away while in my headspace.

His strong lean hand was wrapped in a vice grip around my slim wrist. This wasn't possible before I had come to this house of whispers and sadness. What the hell was going on with my accursed powers? Before, I'd been able to banish all visions and could meditate my way out of almost any escalating situation. Now, here, in this place, I was only a small part of something greater. I had no idea what that was but I didn't like having a new addition to something which already had me on the weird spectrum of life. This is why a simple taste of life would be so wonderful. Simple would save me from insanity. Simple was not what I found at Fenmore Estate.

Chapter Six

Something crawled across the line of our bodies, as he held me firmly. It was invisible but tangible, like the thunder that filled the ozone. He tugged and I rooted myself. In my mental playground, I was standing stock still as I used all of my metaphysical weight to move the objects from my cluttered mind. A part of me knew I was still sitting on the vintage bed but the rest felt as real as being bustled around a crowded mall. This was pushing at my personal space but in a more intimate way.

I reached my other hand out as I tried to pry him off of me, but he countered by grabbing them both.

"No," I informed the dreamed up Kenrick.

He heaved and it was more than I could fight as he was twice my size. I landed against his chest with a thud which knocked the air out of me. It was as if he possessed the magic of a wizard as I no longer felt the pressure of the mattress springs under my legs. Somehow, he had not only kept me from pushing him away but had taken over completely. This had to be my subconscious playing tricks on me because this was just not possible. My body had longed for a safe sexual touch for so long that my brain was more than willing to make the closest handsome male the center of my newly acquired erotic dreams. With this not being in real life, I could submit to some of my needs but giving in would not be like me. Was I truly myself in these queer moments?

My hands were held a yard apart in his flesh covered handcuffs and I only had to look up to see the striking face staring down at me. His eyes were still the focal point, but there was a ghost of a smirk on his arrogant face. As if he knew he had the upper hand in a place that had no physical hands to speak of. I had lost it. Knowing how kooky my life had turned I'd wake up in a padded cell wearing a very snug white jacket with scuffed buckles in the back. At least they would serve me oatmeal and brush the mats from my hair as I drooled and giggled hysterically.

I heard myself whimper, "No" as I didn't want to picture myself in the nut house.

"Yes," he replied.

"Why are you here?" I questioned him as if he was my subconscious needing to explain itself.

"I'm drawn to you."

"I'm not a magnet, so that can't be true. I need to know what the hell is going on."

"Yes, it is as true as any other."

"Any other what?" Confusion had my visions speaking in riddles.

"You are my spider web, my magnet, my pheromone. You have but to flex your will and I am there."

"Bullshit. This is my mind playing terrible games with me and you're a figment of my stress. I can block you out just like I do everything else; I just have to try harder," I said sternly to convince myself.

It was as if my dream was turning into a nightmare because I was too depressed to think happy thoughts.

The fairy tales were correct that you have to force the negative away in every part of your being, mental and physical, in order to be a well-rounded person.

I stiffened my resolve in my mind, even with my hands being held away from me, I squeezed my eyes shut and yelled, *"No!"*

With my eyes so tightly pressed together, I willed him to be gone, but all I heard was the thumping of my heart in the midst of the storm outside my glass window. Then, he laughed, low and seductive. I chanted to myself that this wasn't real. Having no real arm strength, I couldn't get him to let go by yanking so I went to kick him in the groin. Just as the thought turned into action, I was pulled to him in a way that had my body snuggly fitted against his. Again, my mind knew and counteracted.

"Let's see if you can stop this, my dear. Now we test your will and see if you can feel more than my strength against yours with my lust riding across your delicate skin."

I dared not open my eyes as I didn't want to see him in this way. Not with seduction on his wicked tongue. I pleaded for myself to wake up. Wake from this dream that had grown out of simple chemistry for a sexy male. Wake from the temptation which dared to happen. Wake and break the spell before I was a sleeping victim of this want and desire. But all I felt was the press of his lips as the thunder rolled across our bodies.

Such an innocent touch was deceiving. The kiss grew like the air that rolled the center of the storm over us. I had become the central area where the line separated dark from light and prey from predator. I knew which I was and it scared me but not enough to shock me awake. He leaned into me as he pulled my arms to my sides, increasing the amount of our bodies touching. As his arms crept along my ticklish waist, I was yanked the last bit against him where my breasts were a mashed ripeness against his ribs.

I felt his breath exhale over the low-cut cotton of my top and against the skin forced upward from his actions. His arms had mine locked in place even while I tried to pry them loose. I grunted my frustration at him and got a hungrier kiss for my trouble. His mouth slid across mine as if trying to get the flavor of me, like licking the frosting off of a decadent cupcake. This was not supposed to feel good. Damn it.

He nipped at my full bottom lip and got a gasp out of me as his reward. He made a sound of success and slipped his warm tongue into my mouth. This wasn't like any kiss before. This was the cake being devoured, down to every last crumb. I'd never been treated in such a manner. It took me by surprise at how my body wanted to be completely finished off. How could a metaphysical experience be more than I had experienced since losing my virginity at the tender age of nineteen? I'd been in college and had found the moment so lackluster I had avoided the boy at all costs after that. I had even taken a few drinks before the event so I would be less likely to throw myself into a vision at the touch of this very boring man. Both had done the trick as I had been determined to treat it like a business arrangement. Men aren't the only ones who don't call you after a one-night stand. I never even felt guilty for the guy as it had been his first time as well. I saw it as another hurdle that had been taken care of in my life and moved on.

He nipped at me in between lapses of teasing me with his talented tongue. I was so overcome that I had to clench my fists in the fabric of my pajamas to fight grabbing his thighs. I wanted to touch him. And just like that, I got my freaking wish. He let go of my arms and shoved one hand into my tousled hair while the other grabbed my butt cheek. The grip in my hair pulled me to a different angle and caused me to steady myself as I set my hands on his manly hips. My fingernails convulsed into the denim form of him as he squeezed my butt, pushing me into his groin.

Lightning struck near us and a gasp ripped from my surprised form. As I fought for air, he moved to my pale neck and the side that had been free of my hair while he'd gripped my head so tightly. It was just this side of pain, so I didn't fight it. Maybe it was what he had intended, for me to be submissive. Little did he know I wasn't some homegrown virgin. I had needs and he was making me pay attention to them, in small glimpses. The last sexual encounter I had ended with me concentrating so hard on not having a vision the man had called me a dead fish. But how can a girl like me let loose on a man if any strong emotion could throw me into a vision filled nightmare which centered on the man entering you? Celibacy had been my answer, almost two years ago.

I lost my train of thought as he lightly bit my neck. My knees buckled as he hit one of my erogenous zones. He scooped me up and placed me on the bed that magically appeared back into my vision. Instead of my empty headspace, I saw myself back in the bedroom I had at the estate. This time, my legs were too weak to carry me out of there. I let him set me in the middle of the queen sized mattress and surprised myself by staying there as he looked down at me.

"I want to know how you would look under me, Renata."

"Excuse me?"

He leaned down, lying beside me. "Other than acceptance, words are not what I need from you right now."

Then he was kissing me again. Feeling a brief brush of air on my stomach, I realized he was unbuttoning my pajama shirt. Instinctively, my hands were in his hair as he kissed the hell out of me. Before I could come up for air, his hot palm was splayed across one of my naked breasts. He went to nip at my collarbone as his hand went from one eager nipple to the other in a dance over my pale skin. I shivered at the delicate touch of his hands as his mouth ate at the skin of my neck and downward.

His mouth replaced those hands as they swept over my ribs and down to draw circles around my small navel. I was past ticklish and on my way to raw need. I could feel him fumble at my drawstring waistband just as he bit into a taut nipple. My fists clenched around his arms as I fought not to flop on the bed. Once I felt him tug at the string at my hips, I fought the moan that was sure to follow. And it did, as soon as he slipped his talented hand down the front and around my sex. He bit the other nipple and I writhed under him as he took that moment to push a finger inside me.

I was surprised my body was yielding to him as it had been so long since anyone had gotten this far with me. I felt him move around me but dared not open my eyes as he could be gone from this dream with one simple movement. If this was to be a subconscious seduction then I was now a willing participant. There was no clue as to why I could do this but as my body began to sing to me, I couldn't deny myself the simple pleasure of a sexy moment of sleepy surrender. Here there were no fears of a physical touch causing a wicked vision and no chance of regret as it wasn't truly real.

He bathed my aching nipples with his tongue as he swept from one to the other, and then blew across them in a breath which was too cold to come from human lungs. I ached for him. I wanted him fiercely. Basic carnal need was all I could focus on. The booming thunder outside became one with my heart as it fought to release from my rib cage in one bounding leap. If this kept up I would be at the point of begging to have it released for me. Do you ask your lover to cut out the heart which only leaps for them? No, you ask that trusted person to give it wings and you fly together.

He spread butterfly light kisses across my stomach while he used the distraction to pull my pants as low as possible. Once my brain grasped his intentions, I lifted my weak legs just enough for the cotton to be slipped to the floor. Suddenly, I knew there was no going back. I may not have said the words but I had just given my seducer a clear affirmation that I wanted him to take me.

Reaching for him, I began to play my fingertips down the plains of his stomach but he moved away from me. I felt lost for a moment. Why had he stopped me? Then I understood his intentions when he seized my thighs to set himself between them. My soul rejoiced. My nails set into his shoulders as I noticed he had somehow removed his clothes while taking advantage of my limp body. I had no idea how but I was happy to not have the added barrier between us when he pushed his lean frame between my small curvy legs.

His hands were on each side of my face, playing in the hair fanned across the covers. Reaching up, I kissed him, like he'd been kissing me, with fire. Intention. Passion. He had so much strength in his athletic form that he didn't interrupt the kiss to set his groin against mine. The tip of him pushed against my belly and showed me how deep he would be inside of me. I groaned. He flexed and I could tell what he would feel like inside of me. Moving. I wanted that. Now.

Somehow, he knew it. It was as if his joining my dreams made him privy to the dark areas which never saw the light of day. But then again, it was my dream so I'd take the responsibility for this one. The loneliness, the desire, and the need to be accepted as the freak that I am, all of these were fresh and open inside of me. This was truly a dream as I was everything in that one moment between reality and a world of my own making. Here, I could be what I wanted and right now, I wanted to be fucked.

His head slid across me and I shivered with anticipation. Slowly, he slipped into me. It was agonizing how gradually he fit himself inside of me. I wanted to squirm, shake, or throw myself around him. Once he knew this, he chuckled as he pinned my arms above my head.

"Mine, not yours," he whispered into my ear.

The question had to be written across his face as he

replied, "My will, not yours."

As I began to ask more questions, he thrust himself inside of me and I was lost. He gave me a second to take him all in and then set a frustrating pattern. Pulling almost all the way out, he would only slip back in slim increments, teasing me. I was on the verge of yelling at him when he impaled me back onto the bed. Following that with a few more teases, he leaned down to grab a firm nipple in his mouth, bit down and thrust himself so far into me I could feel him at the end of me. That was all it took. I soared.

I shattered so hard that a gasp of unbridled pleasure poured itself out of me before waves of passion had me with my nails deep into his shoulder blades. I was unfastened. Stars were in my vision and he jerked again. I moaned as my core quaked against his manhood in a dance of passion. I was feeling the French death and wanted it. I could die on this pyre. This was a good way to die. If he could remake me, I would allow him to shatter me again and again. In that moment, with the dazzling lights dancing across my vision and the waves of spent lust driving through me, I found a black peace, which welcomed me into its arms. Then all of me slept.

****

A sliver of sunshine pierced through the curtains to spray warmth across my face. Stretching, I began to wake from the best sleep I had had in over a year. Insomnia had been riding side-saddle since I had heard about my job disintegrating. I had taken to hobbies to fill the empty hours when the world was in a dream state. Cross stitch wasn't my thing as it stressed me out at every attempt but I did have success with a couple of knitted shrugs for the days when I had found a few skeins of yarn on the clearance rack. Hobbies on a budget weren't as fun. Books were my main love and why I had liked the small library on the second floor most out of the other rooms in this large house.

I decided I would grab some hot tea and take it to the library and look over the papers again. Laying there, as all my senses began to join in on the day, I got a flashback of my very vivid dream from last night. Oh, my God. I jerked up, in alarm at what I was remembering. I had had hot blooded sex with Kenrick in my dream. *Holy shit!* Looking down at myself, I had to say it was a dream because I was fully clothed and alone in this warm bed.

A part of me was glad I hadn't succumbed to the passion of the very real version of Kenrick Giles but the rest of me wanted it to be as real as the touchable velvet in my room. I wanted to have it as a keepsake I could touch at random and feel the heavy thread of it. A small thrill ran through me as I recalled how quickly he had me burning in flames. I was embarrassed but wondered if it would have been even better in the flesh, instead of in my head. My luck would have turned it into something less sexy and more like a make-out blooper from a B rated scary movie. Women were turned on more quickly when you engaged their minds but this hadn't been a sexy date night full of temptations.

I slid out of the bed and went for a shower before going downstairs for my cup of tea. I hoped to add sugar this time but couldn't remember if there had been any in the pantry. I had been distracted by that creepy door at the time. Somehow, I had gained an appetite overnight. Red meat would have been delicious but I did not believe there would be a rib-eye waiting for me in the camouflaged fridge downstairs. Bacon or some link sausages would be second best, but here was hoping for at least a couple of eggs to scramble up.

Laundry would need to be handled today if I was to keep up with the cooling weather. I was wearing the last of my non-summer clean clothes as I slipped on my flannel lined leggings and the large chambray shirt with corduroy patches at the elbows. It swallowed me as I had lost weight with my dwindling grocery money. My last pair of thick socks were pulled on before I jogged downstairs with a growling belly.

Turning around at the bottom of the staircase, I caught the glint of the green glass as it burnished in the morning rays of the sun as they played against the greenhouse walls. I could go for a walk and investigate the property if the weather stayed this wonderful. It was a welcome after the energy that clung to me from the storm last night. I was surprised I had slept through the majority of it with how tense I had been. It was a good surprise, which didn't happen very often these days.

I put more water in the kettle from last night but was going to turn the heat off just before it screamed good morning to me. While the thin metal heated, I set about looking amongst the grocery items again. There was fresh milk, eggs, and a small slab of peppered bacon in the unit's door. I didn't recall them being there last night but I had been a mess, so anything was possible. Or, there was a slight chance we had a service that brought these things out to us in the farthest part of the district. Shaking my head, it was too convenient to be true for this modern a time.

I was still annoyed at not having Mr. White's

phone number but throwing a three-year-old-like tantrum would not make him show his lined face to answer my growing list of questions. In that case, I set about fixing breakfast. I was able to sip my tea before life was able to shatter my contented silence of the morning. It wouldn't take long to catch up with me as I breathed in the smell of sizzling bacon that was as comforting as the pants I had pulled on this morning. Little pleasures were so important to me these days. They were the rays of sunshine which winked at you behind a dark wall of oppressive clouds.

My mind began to wonder what I could do today, besides take a walk around the sixteen acres of land. I would have to look for property markers as I could easily find myself on a stranger's land. I could look over the sketched map of the estate before I left so I could have a better bearing on which directions were safe to travel. On my way back in, I could grab up some of the tomatoes off of the vine for sandwiches later. If a few were very ripe, then I would see if I had the items to make marinara sauce. Putting down the spatula, I looked back in the dry goods for any pasta and I was happy to see a single package of penne waiting for me there.

Today was falling into place and I felt a little better already. This was a marker of the peacefulness I needed to get myself back to being healthy. Fresh air, solitude, sun-ripened vegetables, all sounded so calm and clear right now. That's what I needed. Not a smug man who could turn me into any knot he could choose. The simple thought had my shoulders tense. Shaking myself back into the now, I pulled the bacon off the stove and slid a plate out. Which was promptly dropped when

Kenrick came into view.

Thank goodness it didn't shatter because who knew if it was something expensive, like most of the items surrounding me. Bending down at the waist, he picked it up and put it on the counter next to the pan of bacon.

"As you've made yourself at home, is there anything left for my own breakfast?"

Picturing that smug face of his meeting the back of the greasy iron skillet was way too good to make reality, so I counted to ten instead. He didn't deserve to see me in jailhouse orange. By the time I hit five, I was smiling but at my imagery of what I wanted to do to him and not his rude way of saying good morning. My wonderful sleep from last night had attributed to me being less aggressive toward my new housemate. The man should consider himself lucky.

"Pardon me. I made myself as comfortable as possible with the little that was offered to me. If I intruded, then I apologize and ask that you simply leave me a detailed list of what I am and am not allowed access to while I stay here."

"You want a detailed list of what you can handle?" he asked with a less stern look on his sexy mouth.

"Yes, as conversation is too much to expect from you, then a list would be helpful."

"Why would you think the conversation would be too much for me? I seem to be handling it rather well at this point. And I can certainly provide you a list, which would be very interesting to put to paper, but I do like a challenge."

Was he flirting with me or simply trying to get me worked into a tizzy?

"You have shown me you are a man of few words.

There has been no discussion of what liberties I am allowed, how I am to get by with my normal daily requirements, or even what is typically done here on a day to day basis."

"Mr. White gave you the general information about what is done on the property, but I was not asked for anything further."

"My humblest apologies, I thought all human beings had the decency to make polite conversation, especially when that person is new to a situation. This is not of my making, but you have also not put forth the effort one would expect if the wheels were reversed," I stammered as I fought to see which emotion the man was aiming for.

"Speak plainly. What are you fussing about?"

I grunted and spun on my feet to move around him. The heck with the spoils of breakfast because he was ruining the gentle atmosphere of my morning with his attitude. I at least wanted my tea before I left him to his snotty tone and pre-made meal. I was filling my teacup and ready to stalk from the kitchen when he rounded on me.

"If you're going to scold me then I would like to know what I did to deserve it."

"You don't know?"

"I am asking. Am I not?"

I harrumphed at him and finished making my cup of tea. As if it would do anything to settle me now. Not unless I could toss it at him, but why waste good tea.

"Mr. Giles, you have not been friendly since I got here. You have not stepped forward to discuss your working knowledge of the property, nor have you said anything to me to make me feel welcome when I have lost the only kind relative left to me. Do you have any emotions in that heart of yours?"

"I happen to be an individual who has things to do and should not have to stop on the account of an unknowing college chick deciding she wants to be on the gothic version of Life of the Rich and Famous."

"What did you just say?" I knew what he'd said but was going to give him a second to backpedal, if he was smart he'd take what I was offering him. I set my cup down slowly, as I really wanted to spray it across his trim jaw then take glee in it spilling from the tips of his shaggy hair.

"I didn't ask to have you here any more than you asked to have your life tossed like a salad. Here is what I have and this is what I have to do to live. Now, if you want to be polite enough to just ask me what you want to know, instead of just expecting me to pull out the estate crystal ball, then go for it, chickie."

"Chickie?"

He just stared at me and I was so flabbergasted I said the only thing that popped into my insane head before the vision hit me like a brick.

"So what, are you going to kiss me now so you can get even with me? Like last night?"

Then I blacked out of reality and into the dark space that showed me the other side of the mirror.

Chapter Seven

I appeared in what seemed to be an attic. A bare bulb hung just behind me and was swinging like an electric pendulum. Peculiar shadows were thrown from the light as I stood in the center of an area that hadn't been used in some time. Dust coated like layers of paint while cobwebs resembled delicate frames for the items displayed before me.

A trunk sat in the eerie darkness as my body's shadow consumed the leather of the vintage exterior. It was the focal point of my vision. I didn't know why but I'd had these long enough to pick up the vibes of power when I'm being pointed toward an object. Tiptoeing over the old rocking horse and the chipped china doll, I stooped to look at the hasp lock before me. There was no extra lock, so opening it would not be difficult. It was a good thing. The bad thing would be what could be in the simple looking trunk.

I didn't know how long I had to see what was being pushed upon me so I bit my lip and gently pulled the lid open. Dust erupted around me, like busy little ants, while my eyes focused to see the contents inside. It was covered in flowered satin but smelled of the pine below the fragile lining. Reaching in, my hands touched the thick binding of a leather book with more cracks than an aged walnut tree. Lifting it was odd as the old tomb was heavier than it appeared. It felt as cumbersome as the sadness which crowded me. Heavier still. A weighty silence that bore witness to many tears.

Then I heard a shriek and breaking glass. Scared, I looked around and found no one. The attic had vanished and my body was back in the kitchen of Fenmore Estate. Later, I would ask myself if it was better to have Kenrick catch me on the way down or if he should've let me hit the cold wood floor. Blinking, I focused on the warmth that surrounded me and not the hardness of the panels beneath me. Kenrick wasn't exactly soft but he wasn't wood with many layers of lacquer on it. Actually, maybe they were the same material and no one had figured out since one had a layer that was much more appealing than the other.

My face was entirely too close to his. It unnerved me how my heart leapt as if I'd been scared out of a horror scene. Some would consider my life to be an ongoing episode of one, with all of the visions and strange happenings. Here I was, in a house from out of Southern Eccentric Magazine, where fluorescent bulbs were more heinous than weeds around the greenhouse and no one would even think to pave the driveway.

Kenrick ran a fingertip across my cheek, reminding me I was staring into his eyes as if under a spell. "Are you all right?"

"Uh. Yes, I think so. It doesn't feel like I hit anything on the way down."

"You do this so often you take inventory when you wake up?"

"Yes. You can let go of me now."

"Let's make sure you're okay before we have you testing gravity again."

He was still touching my face. It was a lazy feeling

and I wondered if this was a way to wake up with someone every day. Not in the way of my visions but as a normal occurrence in my lonely life. With the few dates I've had, and even fewer one-night stands, this was uncharted territory for me. I'd had longer relationships with a vibrator than I did with a flesh and blood man. Then I remembered I had been in his arms last night.

"Okay, enough floor time. I really need that tea now."

"You'll have to get a different cup because you broke the last one."

I peered over his arm and saw the cup I had gotten out earlier was in two pieces a foot away from me. Thank goodness I hadn't fallen on it because I couldn't even begin to tell you where the closest emergency room was to this place. I got up as quickly as possible, even if not gracefully, and scooped the pieces up before Kenrick could stop me. I had them thrown away and was heading back to the cooling kettle by the time he caught up to my actions.

"You're running from me as if I'm the big bad wolf. Why is that?"

I evaded him and grabbed the kettle between us.

"Are you afraid I'll eat you up, my dear?"

"If you'd just flopped onto the floor in front of a stranger, wouldn't you be jittery?"

"But it's not quite anxiety. Or is it? Maybe you're troubled over something a little more touchable."

"Touchable? I'm certain that I felt the floor beneath me."

"But we aren't talking about the floor or the fainting, are we?"

He took a few steps forward and I was close enough to the sink to turn and act as if I needed to get more water, if I could only manage to move. The act would give me permission to turn my back on him but the boogeyman was always there when you turned back around. A light flashed in his eyes. I blinked. It had to be from the reflection of the window. This wasn't some mystery show where the victim saw the gleam of their death in the killer's eyes as the music tempo stepped up. Lord, I was losing it.

Quickly, I turned my back on him and began pouring water into the kettle while I started to babble.

"Do you want any tea? As I recall, my fall interrupted you telling me how rude I was for coming into the kitchen and cooking the food that was here."

"By your tone, I'm guessing you're still perturbed with my choice of words," he said behind me. Was he closer or were my nerves talking?

"A lapse in time does not excuse a lapse in manners, Mr. Giles."

"Now, I'm Mr. Giles?"

His tone was mocking me and I spun on my heel with the water, hoping it would slosh on him. It didn't. Even the water was acting abnormally. Then I noticed he had stepped into the realm of my personal space.

"Excuse me." I avoided his eyes and silently pleaded for him to do as I asked.

"Let's get this settled. Shall we?"

He took the kettle away from me and set it on the burner just behind me. If I had fought then we both would have been soaked. He ignited the burner and I took my advantage by taking a large step away from the man vexing me on almost every level imaginable. He sidestepped and was back to standing in front of me like a choreographed dance.

"Do you mind?" I asked with a small squeak in my voice.

"As a matter of fact, I do. You've been avoiding me this morning and I'd like to know why."

"I have no idea what you're talking about. The only thing I mean to avoid is the rudeness you emanate wherever you go. I've had enough negativity in my life, more of it is just not needed. If ignoring your attitude makes my day better, then I will put my energy into accomplishing that very task."

He folded his arms in front of his nice chest. Well, it was extremely nice in my dream last night, so it didn't hurt to use that adjective. The sex needed a stronger choice of words, but I so wasn't going there when I had the face of this erotic man in front of me. Great, amazing, record-breaking sex. Oh boy. I could feel the heat radiating from my face and wondered what was hotter, me or the kettle on the low flame.

His voice lowered as he bent to meet my hooded eyes. "Why is it you can't seem to look me in the eyes, my dear?"

"I'm not your anything," I realized he had gotten the attention he was looking for. The nerve!

"Why are you bothering me?" I asked him in frustration.

"Am I? Bothering you? That sounds more like a compliment than a complaint."

He had taken another step closer and was now close enough to kiss me. Oh dear. I swallowed. A few times.

Just as his lips inched forward, I squeezed my eyes

shut and fought not to kiss him. This was insane. I popped my eyes back open and began to ramble when the kettle screamed. The screech brought death to the tension-filled moment and I squeaked right behind it.

For the first time in my life, I was thankful for tea. Tea kettles, annoying sounds, screams, and any other deterrent that kept me from making a total ass out of myself. Peeling myself away from the counter to stop the high-pitched noise, I breathed a sigh of relief at being away from the nearness of Mr. Kenrick Giles. The man drew me to him even though his attitude was of an ill-tempered playboy. Maybe, if he'd been less repugnant, I'd have fancied seeing if a kiss would bring visions or just have me wishing I was in a bed somewhere.

Shakily, I fixed my tea and stood in a corner as I went back to ignoring the sexy elephant in the room. He was staring at me from under his tousled hair. It was very predatory, like a tiger wanting to see if I tasted as good as I looked. I couldn't recall a time when I had ever had a man look at me that way. You'd think that among one of my three sexual encounters, one of the gents would have been affected by me. This man wasn't even in a bed with me and I felt like he could eat me up. Well, if dreams were anywhere close to being reality, he could. I'd beg him to.

My mind screamed for me to get the heck out of this room. My tea was just cooling, so I decided to sip it as I walked around the house a bit more. At least, it would give me an excuse to walk away without it looking like I was afraid of him. That's what I was telling myself anyway. Turning, I traipsed out, as if he wasn't burning a hole in me, and forced myself to hum as I walked from room to room, glancing at a few details I hadn't noticed before. Each room had been taken over by a loving hand that knew how to mix a touch of the modern time with the more elegant style of the house itself.

It didn't take long to start noticing my grandmother's touch about this floor. She had a love for lace, rich colors, and comfortable upholstery. I bet she had even picked out the pillows piled on the bed in my room. It soothed me to think of this. This place may have been Mr. Fenmore's but getting a reminder of my own blood filling up this space was an easier way to accept it as a possible home for myself.

Did I want this home? Now that I could see her in it, yes. Before, it felt like a museum that needed a new supervisor. Remarkable how things could change with just a turn of the mental wheel. It would be overwhelming to see the day to day items I would have to add to my life if I accepted this home. But seeing as I would have the finances to focus on that task, it could be managed. If taking this leap allowed me to be a part-time worker, then I could add my career as a side income for anything personal I needed. A car would be one for the list in the near future. I loved my old girl but maybe I could donate her to someone who could fix her up right. I'd have to check into it.

Being out here, I only had a couple of neighbors and most didn't seem to be involved in the estate or I might have seen them while I was here. Normally, a good old-fashioned neighbor would come by to see if anything was needed when you lost someone in the community. No sign of that here, so I could continue my introverted lifestyle. Why was it so comforting? Did

I want to be part of this town since I was such a basket case? Or would I turn into a hermit with a hundred cats ghosting around the tree-lined property? The thought made me giggle into the empty hall as I made my way back to the kitchen for my last cup of hot tea.

The room was empty but it hadn't been for long as I noticed a terry tea cozy had been slipped onto the steaming kettle. The dishes had been cleaned and there were two blueberry muffins lying on a saucer by the range top. If it was an apology, then I would accept it. Reaching for a fruit-laden muffin, I saw a note scrawled under the delicate saucer. Picking it up, I studied the masculine scrawl neater than any man's I had seen in my life. It held the characteristics of a time long ago with parchment and ink quills.

Take this token for my poor choice in words this morning. I'm not used to guests, only Mr. Fenmore, so I should have minded my manners. I will be heading to town for a few more food items but not until after my morning chores are finished. I'll stop by when I clean up and see if you have left a list of anything you may need for the next day or so. It will go on the account, so no money will be needed. If you can stomach my company, I would like to cook dinner for you tonight. If this is agreeable to you, please state what time would be acceptable.

Til then,

KG

The note took me a bit to digest. Not only had he apologized, but he was doing a few nice things to correct the situation. There were a couple of items I could use from the store but felt bad for the estate having to cover it. The small amount of cash I had in my bag was for gas and emergency purposes, as there was nothing in my bank account. I found the pen in the drawer by the silverware and wrote down a couple of items that shouldn't be a problem. Did I want to have dinner with him? It seemed intimate after the near-kiss scene earlier. But not as sexually intimate as my dreaming that he made love to me last night. If that was what you could call it. Could I make it through an actual meal with my face burning like the fires of hell? Any nun would have my hide for even thinking some of these thoughts, let alone my dreams. Thank God, I wasn't Catholic. I had grown up with one friend who had been and she'd turned tail and run at my first vision. She had said only children of the devil had such insight. My grandmother had been the only person in the family accepting of my curse. She said the little girl had been impressionable and had not understood the rules of the church. That may have been so, but it showed me I was an outsider at a very early age and that some blamed religion for their own fears.

If I could get through those moments, then I could have a civilized dinner with a man who was positioned as a partial host to me while I was on the property. He'd be the only person with an insight into the dealings around the estate, so I might as well take his olive branch. I replied that anywhere after five would be great, as I knew light would be limited if we made it any later. He could make his decision from there as to what he wanted to prepare. I also replied that I had no food allergies and knew it was one less thing he would have to consider.

I wasn't going to dress up for dinner, as it would seem as if I was trying to attract his attention. I would just wear jeans and my nicest long-sleeved shirt. That would mean I would have to find the laundry room soon since I was out of fresh apparel. I'd already resorted to washing my underwear in the sink, so it was a bonus. Being out here, I needed a few pairs of corduroy and maybe a couple of wool items. I had been accustomed to wearing several thin layers of summer clothes as I had worked at the warehouse, but that may not be enough. One could imagine the wear and tear on a wardrobe when you worked in an old metal and brick building while refinishing and recovering all ages of furniture. I liked getting my hands on dingy old pieces and ripping them back to life. It was fulfilling, even if a lowly paid job. Most of my clothes were plain dark colors and made of cotton. No fancy fabrics for me and more affordable.

Eating my peace offering, I sipped at the last bit of tea while I scouted for a washing machine. Thankfully, there was an older set in a laundry room hidden away at the back of the house. In the shelf above it was enough cleaners for the laundry and the entire house. One less thing to worry over. There was also a small freezer in the room with several different sizes of frozen meat carefully labeled as to when they had been stored and what was in the meticulously wrapped packages. When you are in an area still being used for farming, it wasn't a surprise that two of the ones up front were venison.

I would have liked to look on my old smartphone for a weather report but there was no internet connection in here. It would explain why I didn't see any televisions in any of the rooms either. That library was looking better and better to me. A list would need to be made for the items I wanted to upgrade around the estate, like the internet, to see if it was allowed within the eccentric rules of my step-grandfather. If the internet company didn't have to tear anything up, or leave it in a tacky mess, then I would hope it would be acceptable. Especially, if I was going to try to work from here in my own refurbishing business. T.V. Shows were overrated but I'd like to have at least a house line and enough internet to do basic research and emailing.

I ran upstairs to get my laundry, since I was alone and knew he wasn't using it, and then set a load on. While the clothing was washing, I decided to check out a few other places in the house. Maybe I'd find a few more points of interest to use as small talk at dinner this evening. Running some of my inquiries for Mr. White by Kenrick could save me some time but it might also drive him back into being more sullen. Why was I even bothering? I had no idea but I actually wanted this to go well. I was stuck here and he was the only person I knew in this area unless you counted Mr. White, and I didn't.

Meandering around the rooms that I had already glanced over, I decided to walk around the unexplored third floor. The halls were all dark, from the lack of sunshine peeping under the closed doorframes. My hesitancy at opening a private room reminded me there was no one else living here to take offense at my unwary entrance. There was no solid proof that Kenrick even slept in this house, so it was the closest I would get to anything personal. Hearing no noise on this floor, after holding back on the top of the stairs, I pushed my feet forward. If a door was unlocked, then I would enter. If it was locked, I could ask my dinner companion about it this evening.

There were seven doors down the silent hallway and none of them were open in invitation. This seemed to embody the feeling of the whole house in one slim walkway. Opening the first door, I was enveloped by the subtle shades of navy blue and deep gold in what looked to be a seldom used spare bedroom. A faint layer of dust was upon the heavy mahogany furniture. It was impersonal, with no items of distinction lying about or even a picture hung on the elaborate wallpaper but it was a room of cool comfort.

On the opposite side was a restroom and a small linen closet before another bedroom designed in a rose pattern with cherubs on the dainty wallpaper. It was purely feminine and almost doll-like in its charm. By the blue room was a broom closet with a water heater and a large spider web that had me shudder for the size of the spider that had to have made such a large design of vulnerable lace. The last two doors were at the very end of the hall with one on each side. I was more leery about opening these doors. I had no reason for the creeping along my spine but I had to acknowledge it was there. But what energy was I picking up and who had left a lingering piece of it in this part of the house?

The last door on the left swung open easily and the interior caught my breath. There were no dust or cobweb frames in this lovely room. What I found was a whitewashed room with an intricate canopy bed painted in unrelieved black. The detailing was a mass of pointed arches and mitered wood. It looked like someone had used the interior of a gothic cathedral to make a king-sized bed. The thick covers were a chocolate brown that begged to be touched. I never would have pictured the reversed color scheme to be so appealing but it was gorgeous. Both the ornate dresser and nightstand were in the same black but with more modern tan and black lamps.

That's when I noticed the shirt lying over the back of a brown high back chair by the closet. It was the one Kenrick had been wearing yesterday. I had been clutching that shirt when I'd had the vision on the front landing. I was intruding in his private space and thank heavens he wasn't here to witness my gawking. If he'd been in here, no matter the state of undress, then I would have probably raced for the security of my locked bedroom door. I even had to stop myself from looking in the closet as that was just crossing the line. Forcing myself back to the door, I prayed he wouldn't see me sneaking out of his room.

Exhaling the breath I had been holding, I made my way across the hall and to the last door left unopened. It creaked with the age of the house and led to a choking space of age and dust. It was as if the combined years of the estate lay in the confines of this small room. This was the attic space from my vision. I hated it when the images were in full blooming color in front of me.

Chapter Eight

The attic must have been the whole floor at one time but renovations had it narrowed down to this extension of the house. It was exactly like I had pictured it. A dress form stood with a withered feather boa wrapped around it, like an antique store mannequin. The old wood flooring was lined with trunks, chairs in need of repair, and tables of all sizes. This room would make a refurbishing queen cry and I was such a woman.

So many exquisite pieces and all I could focus on was the trunk I had seen earlier in my vision. Was it really in here? Tiptoeing around the room of elder furniture, I used my growing night vision to see as much as possible. Thank goodness I hadn't closed the door behind myself or I would have already tripped over a priceless piece of history. I would've cried if I'd done irreparable damage to one of these beauties.

Centering myself, I went back over the mental image of the trunk I had found. It was varnished a dark brown with leather straps that buckled it closed. There was no padlock on the one from my mind, so I hoped I had the same luck with the real one. Recalling the items around it, I swung about to see where those pieces were located. Sure enough, I was looking at the dresser that was right beside the trunk from my memory. Sometimes I hated how creepy this metaphysical stuff worked out.

I settled myself on my knees in front of this Pandora's Box and prayed this wouldn't make my life worse. Slowly pulling the lid wide, I noticed there were several items inside. Sifting through age riddled photos and yellowed linens, it took a few minutes before I found the sturdy leather item I was searching for. It was weighty and had an ageless aura about it. It seemed to vibrate with its own life source. This was no ordinary book. This contained a whiff of magic mixed with a taste of the otherworld. My skin crawled at the touch of energy which recognized my curse. Yes, anything that keeps a person from getting laid was not to be considered a blessing.

Thumbing the clasp open, I flipped open the cover to see the name *Aster* scrolled in bold calligraphy across the first page. Flipping through a few more pages, it seemed to be a diary from about a hundred years ago. Most intriguing. I decided to take this to my room for reading. I might be brave enough to roam around someone's house but diaries were more personal. I needed to get out of here without being noticed. And as luck would have it, I heard steps on the staircase.

Quickly, I closed the attic door before standing silently behind it. I was holding myself as still as the grave when I heard the steady thump of his shoes on the long wood floor of the hallway. The air was quiet as if waiting for me to exhale and give my hiding place away. My lungs would burst if he didn't move soon. Just when my body began to scream for air, he shuffled to his room and the door clicked shut. Drooping against the solid door, I caught my breath and paused as I waited for the best time to tiptoe away.

As this might be my home, I shouldn't feel as if I had to lurk in the shadows. Damn it, I felt like a teenager who had been caught stealing booze. Straightening my shoulders, I stiffened my spine and took a step toward the stairs. A sigh of relief escaped me as I finally sat on the covers of my made bed with the book in a stiff grip. The leather was slightly faded and worn, as if used to being carried around for decades. Curious, I opened it to the first page and wondered who Aster was. On the back of the inside of the cover was a scrawled date, March 1907. It really was a hundred years old. It was the end of February now. What a coincidence? A small piece of me laughed hysterically at that thought. It must be from my slip of paranoia from being almost busted upstairs.

Looking at the clock, I had spent two hours rambling around the third floor. I still had lunch to deal with and about four more hours before I headed down for my dinner appointment. This girl wasn't going to casually pine away in her room as she waited for her gentleman caller to show up. It wasn't that kind of evening and I certainly wasn't that type of girl. Sadly, I realized a romantic date would be wonderful for my morale. My decision was to read a few pages before grabbing something light for my lunch then I'd take another walk around the property. Maybe in a year I would know the property better, if I kept it.

Kicking off my shoes, I tucked my legs under myself and flipped the page. It was indeed a diary. There was a date of birth, October 31, 1886, below the name Aster Edwards but under it was the date January 1907. That meant she was twenty-one when she had written in this diary. Back then, they had Harry Houdini and Teddy Roosevelt in the headlines. I liked historicals, even if not from such a recent time, so maybe it was something romantic. Yes, I was romance deficient. I could at least admit it to myself.

She was home from her chores and discussing a young man who she was enamored with. She described him as lovely, which I giggled at. Few men could be called that unless they were more feminine in looks and presence. Modern women would be more likely to use the term attractive metrosexual. Aster went on about how much of a gentleman he was but that she wanted to see him in a more aggressive fashion. Maybe she wanted him to make a move on her or she thought he was too sedate for her. That last one would account for the term of lovely. It went further to where she was so infatuated with him I surmised she wanted to be seduced by this man.

My sensibilities shouldn't be shocked as ladies my age were walking around with condoms in their purses. But somehow the age of the diary had me thinking of chastity belts and men being run out of town on horses. It was wrong of me and I had to let go of these images as I continued to read her story. It went on with her devising a plan to make the guy show more interest in her. Sad to say that women still did this over a hundred years later and I was not immune to this problem. Aster stated she had the looks to gain his attention but all of her subtle hints were being ignored. It seemed to have her irritated since she couldn't understand how he hadn't fallen for her charms already.

Well, she sounded a bit conceited to me. As I was far from beautiful, I became used to being ignored after the initial look over. Yes, it hurt my feminine pride but

I knew there were better-looking people everywhere I went, especially as even the pre-teens were getting nose jobs and breast implants. I'd love to have luscious full breasts but I hadn't been graced in puberty or in my bank account. I shrugged it off and knew I was just the right size to wear a push-up bra or to go without, depending on the garment. It was a blessing and a curse, just like my visions.

Aster went on about other guys who found her tempting but this particular one, nicknamed "G", was going to notice her one way or the other. Did all young women sound this way? I hoped to God I never did, but then again, I couldn't get laid without seeing the man in a sex stopping vision. I thanked my stars I couldn't read minds too. That would just have me in the sanitarium for the rest of my old cat lady days. I was beginning to wonder if this girl was just playing out a drama in her head as I found her harder and harder to believe. She wasn't giving the name of the guy, where she'd met him, what he did, or even what he looked like. Weren't we females notorious for oversharing info on guys we were crushing on? In school, I was a babbler when my first crush had even met eyes with me across the gymnasium. This small detail told me she was hiding information, a piece of herself, away from the world at large.

After another thirty minutes of her ranting and plotting, I set the book down and slipped back into my discarded shoes. Aster was so full of herself she didn't need a man to show her any more attention than what she got out of her own mirror. Her thoughts were grating on my nerves and I didn't need that, so I headed outside. The air was brisk, with an icy edge to it that told a tale of the upcoming winter season. In the south, it came to us around this time of year and even into the first week or two of March. I bet it was beautiful here when covered in a layer of snow like vanilla icing on the estate grounds. Its own winter wonderland, especially as I didn't know my way around it yet.

Walking mindlessly over the brown tipped grass, I encountered a water fountain that was graceful in its architecture but more like the dessert as it hadn't seen a fresh flow of water in many moons. Looking more closely at the dug-out area, I could see where stones had been set in a semicircle around the fountain. Most of the stones were tumbled or broken but you got a glimpse of a delicate sitting area that had been here around the same time the house had been built. An even closer look showed some of the stones were, in fact, some of the same decorated ones as the ones by the front entrance to the house. This would be a great restoration that I could do when the weather was a bit warmer. Wait, I was already making plans and hadn't even signed the papers.

Shaking my head, I kept wandering on and there seemed to be a path from several years back. The outline of it was there against the dying weeds that had once been fluffy dandelions. Bending over to grasp a handful of the limp shoots, a stiff wind came from nowhere and I lost my balance in the surprising gust. The air around this place seemed to just shove you aside and was the most rude piece of nature I had witnessed since being here. If it was solid, then I would ask the presence what I had done to offend it so strongly. But the wind was not for long discussions. It was one of whispers and tickles in the briefest of moments.

That's when I viewed the headstones. Focusing my eyes on the number of them, it was a cemetery with a huge weeping willow guarding it against the normal view of anyone coming around this side of the yard. In the summer, this area would be hidden from anyone unknowing of this family resting place. Another breeze came through and brushed over the tangles of the tree limbs. It made a sound like muted bamboo chimes as they beat against each other in the unexpected onslaught. Dusting off my butt, I made my curious way over to the stone circled area. A finger of awareness crept down my spine as I crossed the threshold of the holy section of ground.

Power always acknowledged power, no matter how subtle. A prayer was murmured from my tense lips as I pushed through that sensation and moved onward to see the names on the headstones. The more ornate ones were for the first generation of the Fenmore family with the small ones set deep into the grass being other names not familiar to me. I wondered if it was servants or people who had married into the Fenmore family. Maybe I could find a bible with the names of all involved in the family amongst the items in the attic.

In the very back corner was a stone buried under an overgrowth of weeds. This set me back a bit as I could clearly read the names on the other stones and wondered why someone had completely left this one uncared for. A current pushed at me again and it was hard enough for me to wobble as I fought for balance. It may not have succeeded in downing me but it blew some of the debris away as if blowing out a birthday candle. Stooping, I swiped at the layers of crusted earth to see the name had been scratched off as if no one wanted this grave to be known. A very disconcerting thing to see. The spine jolt came back when I placed my palm flat on the desecrated granite at my feet. I was swooped into another vision and this one hurt. It was as if a filet knife was being yanked down between the layers of my tingling skin and the ungiving bone of my spine. Crying out with the pain that emanated, I fell into another mental episode from the past.

The diary was in the arms of a slim woman. I could tell this by the view of her side where the book was nestled under her arm at her right hip. There was no face to her. It was as if I was the lady and was looking down at her prized possession. Her feelings were clear to me, in my head. She had found something she was certain would get her the one thing she wanted above all else. Having already made a deal with the devil to get this wish, she was entirely committed to seeing it become reality.

She was looking at the greenhouse and I heard her slip of mirth as it escaped her curved lips. This young lady was wearing a simple white sundress but with a wool scarf around her shoulders. She could feel the chill seep into her but her mood would not be downed as she'd finally found the link she needed. She was boiling over in her self-satisfaction, like a feline that could see the mouse in its growling belly. The cat in her would put out the cheese and wait for her unknowing victim. It was hard for her to wait the three days it would take for things to be lined up but she was confident of her skills. I could see a shadow move along the green glass of the greenhouse but not who was working behind those tinted windows.

My host began to sing a French song to the shadows she was embraced in. She lurked under a tree in the yard, while no one was looking for her. If her father found out she was skipping out on her chores, he'd deny her the money she needed for her supplies. She swung around and scanned the yard to see if she would be caught peeping at her prey. Seeing the misty version of the estate house behind her, no one was walking about. She was safe to make her way back to the front where she had been tending the flower beds the lady of the house adored so much. No one knew some of the plants were not in the plans but of her own choosing. These were special. In three days, they would join her shopping list items and would be put to their proper use. Finishing her whispered song as she gazed once more at the greenhouse, she tiptoed back to the front of the house where her bag and her chores awaited her.

My lungs screamed for air as I came to find myself lying upon the grave like a mourning loved one. Dirt and debris were a fine layer upon me as I slowly got to my feet, dazed. The pain slowly ebbed away as I brought my senses back to the present. Whoever that lady was, she had a grudge against someone. I felt sorry for the person in her sights as I could taste her anger on my tongue like raw vinegar. Turning to look back at the house, her version of it was a newer image where my distant one was more weathered and broken in. She'd been here when the trees were younger and the greenhouse had been built on. I'm guessing it was about eighty years ago as I recalled her clothing and the newness of the leather book. I gasped as I realized the book in her arms had been the diary that had called to me from the attic. So, it had to be Aster that I was hosted by.

The psychological insights from her diary made sense as she was a woman scorned. It didn't make her sane but it made me feel that she wanted satisfaction from the person who had hurt her pride. If she'd been more mature then she could have simply talked to the person from the greenhouse or she could have seen her way to letting go of the negativity that was bleeding into her soul like cancer to a sick child. The scene had me more intrigued with what I would find on the next day's listing in the diary if there was one. I had stopped at the end of the first long day when it had prattled on and on about the wrong she needed to have made right.

Making my way back to the house, after dusting my body off, I would have to cleanse the cling of the dead off of me when I got to my room. I'd have to make a stop in the laundry room and hope my load was dry but I just couldn't bear the thought of her decaying form on my sensitive skin. I wasn't old-fashioned but my curse knew it had been caressed by another and I had to stop the feeling of that anger filled link. Maybe a cup of chamomile tea would soothe me after I got cleaned up. I hoped so because I felt like a traveling case for the train of souls as I shuddered from the memory of the vision riding my mind. Anyone in the field of death had heard the rumors of grave dust being used for dark magic and I didn't want to find out if it could turn into something tangible. No, not this girl.

At the door, I noticed my shoes had a layer of debris and dust on them. Slipping them off, I twisted the doorknob open and got my eyes to begin the adjustment to the lack of light in the front rooms. It wasn't dark, per se, but it wasn't as bright with the sun to the back of the old house. The kitchen would be warm and cheery at this time of day, which would be comforting when I sat down to have dinner with Kenrick. I had two hours before I needed to be back down here so I tucked my shoes under my arm and headed to the utility room for my clothing. That one load was waiting to be dried as I realized I hadn't waited long enough to put it in the dryer before I had gone on my walk. It left me with nothing to wear after my shower and before my dinner date. I was not about to have him find me this way but I was at a loss for what to wear while my jeans and three shirts were tumbling in the heat.

Fumbling around the shelves and behind the door, I didn't see anything other than a cheery blue paisley apron that was more for looks than for actual heavy duty cooking. I was not about to have my fanny sticking out like a nudist in a cooking show. I giggled but just couldn't see myself doing it on purpose, even if it was large enough to almost touch in the back. My rear would be visible in an eye-catching slip of two creamy inches. I blushed at the mental image and finished my task of turning on the dryer before I headed back to the front door where I could bang off some of the debris. I'd have to run a soapy cloth over them once I was in the restroom. Jogging upstairs with my shoes jostling under my arm, I prayed there was a sheet or a towel large enough to cover up with once I got the ick off me.

I plopped my shoes by the tub and started running the water. It would have to be a short one as I was not liking the idea of having the grave dirt in the bathtub with me. The thought was unnerving as I pictured the particles as souls floating in the River Styxx. I stopped the water and changed my mind. A sponge bath would be sufficient and I didn't need all that water to freak me out. I saw a bottle of lavender oil under the sink and a towel large enough to get all the way around me. My tiny ray of hope shined. Terry cloth would make me a more decent sight for the man that could run through the hall at any given moment and the oil to soothe my raw nerves.

Hot fragrant water lapped around my calves as I folded myself into the tub and began sloshing water over my skin. Trying not to think of where the grime came from, I hummed a tune to distract myself. It didn't take long to feel better about my rinsed skin, and I grabbed the towel for a quick rub down. I squeezed my hair in the towel and was just securing the edges together when I heard my name being called from the hallway. If I answered, would he try to come in or would he stay away? Did I want to risk it? Peeking my head out the doorway, I went for middle ground.

"I'm not decent. Whatcha need?" I asked and kept my voice neutral.

"Oh, I'm going to go pick up some things and will be back in an hour to start fixing dinner."

"Okay. Thanks for letting me know," I replied awkwardly.

I saw his shadow as he paused at the top of the staircase. Did he want to come up the hallway? I hoped not as I probably looked dreadful.

I heard the floorboard creak as he turned to go back down the steps and then him opening the front door. The question hit me that I hadn't seen a car yet. I'd ask him about it later because I certainly wasn't running out there right now. Going to my room, the lavender was comforting on my flesh. That and the borage of visions had me thinking of a nap. Never being where I could indulge myself like that, I thought what the heck. I wasn't hurting anyone and had no plans for a little while.

Having made my decision, I plopped down the shoes I had cleaned up in the bathroom and tossed the towel over the radiator by the door to the hallway. Tucking myself between the cool sheets made me shiver but it didn't take long to radiate enough warmth to take the chill away. I stopped my mind wandering over the events of the day, this morning and this evening. If I didn't then I'd be awake for days and that was just asking for trouble. The few nights I stayed awake for exam cramming had turned into three days of back to back visions which had me wanting to slam my head into a broad brick wall. Being in a coma would have been preferred to seeing every single past experience from the few people I had touched in the halls on campus. It had been horrifying. I knew more about them then I did about my own grandmother.

Once cleared, my mind let me sink into the depths of a quiet open space where I was always safe. The white noise was created by my forcing my mind to push activity out in waves. They rolled over me and I forced myself to absorb the sensation. It was like squinting your eyes shut so tightly that you see spots, but with my hearing. Concentrating, I heard the steam coming from the towel drying on the radiator. It was soothing. It pushed me down further, under a blanket of peace. Feeling a brush of steam across my cheekbone felt wonderful as I turned my head into the warmth of it. Inhaling, I took in the smell of fresh cotton and cut wood. That wasn't what it was supposed to smell like. Not wanting to open my eyes, I felt it again and forced myself to comply. I'd probably never get back to sleep now. Swallowing my gasp, I saw Kenrick leaning over me.

Chapter Nine

"What the fuck are you doing in here?" I grasped the cover to my thumping heart.

"I'm not," he responded with a ghost of a grin.

"Yes, you are," I replied.

"No, you're dreaming again."

Was I? He sounded so sure, like it'd be crazy not to believe him.

"I'm not asleep. I was *trying* to when you waltzed in here and overstepped your bounds. If you feel bad about it then you can let me get back to it."

"You are most certainly dreaming and I can prove it to you," was his comment as he stayed right over me.

"How are you going to do that, by disappearing into thin air?"

"I'm going to kiss you and you'll kiss me back."

I barked a laugh at him. "How is that going to prove anything?"

"If you were awake and I had indeed had the indecent thought to come in here and seduce you, I believe my body would be on the floor in a broken heap."

"You've got that right," I tried to sound convincing.

"Then what is your worry? If this is a dream, no damage has been done. If it's real then you have my permission to do with me what you like."

The devilish gleam in his eyes turned his sentence to a more sexual line of thinking. Did I believe it to be true, that I was having another sexy dream? I'd had one earlier so it was possible. I'd also experienced enough visions to have loads of mental issues messing with my state of being. Something inside of me truly accepted his reasoning. Pinching myself, it hurt but the image before me didn't change. I was still naked in bed with a handsome man leaning over me like I was his next meal being served on the table. My body went hot and cold all at once.

"You pinched yourself in a dream? Does that ever really wake anyone up?"

"You're being damned calm about all of this."

"Being a dream has its advantages, my dear."

He just watched me. It was disconcerting.

"Fine. Just a kiss and then you can go invade someone else's dream," I gave into the insanity of my subconscious.

Was there a glimmer in those sexy eyes? Dreaming, I reminded myself. When those lips touched mine, I lost the battle of my inner desires. Just that simple, I wanted him. Last time, he was more delicate in his actions. Not this time. He'd already had a taste and I was now something to devour. His tongue pushed forward and took possession of the lonely emptiness. Letting go of my grip on the covers, I grabbed a handful of his soft wispy hair and used it to pull him down onto me. It took a moment to become comfortable under his masculine frame but a chuckle vibrated from his chest while I squirmed for a moment. I could feel a grin on the mouth happily glued to mine.

Sliding my eyes down his lean body, I saw jean-clad legs, bare feet, and a black t-shirt. Yummy. Why did the sight of his naked feet make my stomach flip? Was it the intention behind it knowing this was the type of man who was always seen fully clothed during daylight hours? It just worked for me. If he'd been in sweatpants then I might have started foaming at the mouth. But my lips wanted something more substantial than white foam. They wanted to slide across every part of this devilish man. Twice. The urges in me right now were foreign to my stale love life, shockingly so. If I was going to have any more of these dreams, then I would try to take care of a majority of them. Why not when it was all in my fantasy riddled head.

I kissed him like I was starving and I was. When he lifted his head, I felt bereft and breathless. I wasn't so bothered when I noticed it was so he could remove his cotton shirt. He may not be a mountain of manly muscles but his lean body had hills and valleys like a man who took great care in his health. If this happened to be a farmer build then sign me up for a few days in a field for some ogling bliss. My fingertips explored that expanse by instinct alone. His body was a bit cool but that might be because I felt like combusting against this man as he drove me to wanting an eye-rolling orgasm of epic proportion. And my body knew he could give me the tickets to fly.

His lips met mine but he hadn't set himself back against my chest. I peeked an eye open and saw he was holding himself up on one arm as the other grabbed the comforter which covered my naked breasts from his view. Slowly peeling it back, he pulled it down to my waist. A shiver ran over my exposed skin as anticipation built instead of paying attention to the warmth being taken away from me. The look in his eyes was dark enough to hide in as he peered down at my pale breasts. Biting back an apology for my lack of voluptuous curves, I waited for the disappointment to show on his face. It didn't. As a matter of fact, I couldn't see his face fully because he was sucking one of my budded nipples into his lava warm mouth.

Moaning, I shut my eyes and dropped my head back to the pillows. He was hungry at the meal of my flesh. He scooped as much of one perky breast into his mouth as he could, teeth scrubbing into the tender flesh, and sucked until I felt liquid run down to my core. I'd never had this done to me before. Sure, a guy or two had fondled my boobs during a hot goodnight kiss but not to this extent. The attention he paid to them had me glad to be the size I was graced with. Any more and he couldn't have gotten it all in his mouth and too little would have given me less of a sensation of him pulling my need out of my body with every tug of his tongue. He did the same to the other side and I about came off the bed as my moan slipped up my throat.

My hands were fisted in his hair by the time he was done there and I forced myself to loosen my grip as he pulled his face down to my navel. I would have never thought of it as a sensitive area but the way he nipped at it had me wishing he was much lower with that talented mouth of his. He slid off of the bed, with his teeth biting tenderly into the mound of my soft belly and I almost slipped down with him as I didn't want his touch to stop. Hearing him fumbling around, I turned to see him undoing his jeans as he kneeled over the bed. He was adept at his skills as he laved over the tissue he had made hypersensitive with his attention. His eyes met mine and he let go of me as he stood up and let his pants shimmy down his strong legs. There was no underwear in sight so he'd either gone commando knowing he'd be in my room or he'd been crafty enough to shed them with his jeans. Scanning down the length of his male form, I was delirious with the way my dream was turning out.

Surprising me, he slid a hand under the blanket, lightly tickling my hip, before he cupped my crotch. As I looked at him in surprise, he swooped down to kiss me with even more heat than the one before. I ran my fingers over his nipples as he moved his mouth to nip at my neck and shoulders. While he distracted me here, his slightly calloused fingers were pulling my right leg closer to the edge of the bed. He traced the length of my leg, from toe to thigh, once he had it settled over the edge beside his bent form. I shuddered when his hand cupped me again, molded to it. I wanted more and he was experienced enough to know it. Taking a rose pink nipple between his front teeth, he flicked his tongue over it several times as his hand went where I wanted it. And I did. I was in a frenzy of need, like never before. He had my body coming alive at his slightest touch. Then he ran a finger over the cleft of my sex. I gasped and he sucked my nipple so hard I cried out as he slipped a finger to rub across the nub of me, making my spine bow.

He kept the area covered as he drove me to madness at not getting this tangible craving fed. Another flick of my nipple and a finger entered me. When he thrust his finger in like it was a vibrator, I bit into one of my flailing hands to keep from screaming. After a few pumps, another finger joined the first one and I did scream. He pulled and twisted his hands as he worked to find every spot he could in the center of me. Writhing, I clenched a hand around the muscles of his arm and dug my short nails into that column of flesh like a lifeline. I wanted to grab his dick but he evaded me. I put my hand back on his arm and held on. My bitten hand went to brace myself on the side of the bed, clenching like I'd fall off of a cliff. That's how I wanted to die, deep in the hold of passion.

Just when my whimpering grew, he threw the covers off my form and landed between my still open legs as my shock took hold of his quickness. Then he thrust into me with knowledge of where to hit, and I was gone. My eyes rolled into my head, and I grasped him to my heaving chest. I would burst if he stopped. I would throw myself off the roof if he faded away at this point of my dream. I needed him to release me or I would die without it. With him pounding into me, I ran my nails down his sides before gripping his firm buttocks. He groaned, and I squeezed so hard my knuckles ached against him. I stayed where I was as he moaned into my gasping mouth. Then he rolled his hips and I came with my heart exploding against him. I writhed as he kept moving before finally joining me in my wild abandon. I flew and his arms were there to catch me as I sailed onward.

****

Distantly, I began to absorb the sounds of movement on the floor under me. It was muted but enough to remind me there was someone in the house besides myself. Peeling my eyes open to look at the clock on the mantel, it read 5:15, and the person scurrying around must be Kenrick cooking us dinner.

Inhaling, I caught a scent of lemon pepper and knew I had to get up and head downstairs.

Flinging the covers off of myself, the breeze had me shocked to remember I had lain down without dressing which was unusual for me. Then the rest of my slumber session came into view and I about fell off the rumpled bed. Cheeks burning with the flame of one hundred virgins, I fumbled for clothing to wear and remembered they were in the dryer downstairs, with Kenrick. *Shit!* Now I had to decide on either wearing a towel down there or putting grave dusted cotton back on my clean body. The last one had me shuddering from the lingering psychic connection with the grime rubbing into my pores. No, I wasn't putting that back on.

Noting my remaining options, I could call him up here and see if he could bring them to me, leaving me vulnerable again. Did I venture down there in a towel and hope he believed me when I said I'm only down there to get clean clothes? What red-blooded man would see it that way when a lady walked in barely covered by terry cloth? How did I get myself into these situations? Had I not gotten my dose of living awkwardness when born with this curse of visions? If God only gave you as much as he thought you could take, then he and I needed to go back over my job duties. I needed better insurance or maybe even hazard pay.

Swathing myself in the warm towel from the radiator, I slowly peeked out my door to see if anyone would witness this unusual walk of shame. Astonishment shot through me when I took in what lay on the floor of the hall just outside my room. My jaw dropped. There my clothes were, all folded, and waiting for me to put them in a drawer. Had he come across mine as he went to do his own laundry? I didn't tell him I had to wash clothes and he hadn't seen me when I'd come up here covered in death dust. Or had he? He knew I'd gotten in the shower but there was no proof of my forgetfulness in my duties. It was just creepy, even if a Godsend for me not having to go down there in this getup.

Holding onto the tucked edge of the towel, I used my free hand to scoop up the pile and quickly ducked back into my room before I flashed anyone. Thunder rumbled in the distance as I yanked on the first pair of jeans and flannel shirt in the stack. My hair was a tousled mess and the coming rain would probably make it grow to chia sized proportions if I didn't at least run anti-frizz gel into it before flopping down the stairs. In a bit of girly pride, I added a smudge of deep purple eyeliner and my lip-gloss. I wasn't going to do more and make this man think I'd been in here primping for him this evening. Tossing on my only other wool socks, I realized this would have to complete my attire as my shoes were still a bit damp. Setting them closer to the radiator, I smoothed my hair down one last time before I jogged down the steps and to my undate like dinner appointment.

Almost slipping off the last step and colliding with the hall table, I recovered enough to hear my name being called from the kitchen. Deep breath taken, I casually moved forward. Forcing a pleasant smile to my lips, I walked in and took in the image before me. There was a man humming an old Sinatra tune and cooking at the stove in jeans, bare feet, and a black t-shirt. It was like he'd jumped right out of my wet dream and straight into the job of making me a sandwich. I was in the process of shutting my jaw when he spoke again.

"Renata, what are you doing?"

Letting go of my face, I fidgeted at being caught at such a silly gesture. He wouldn't know I was trying to pull myself from the heated land of dreaming.

"So, Chef Giles, what will we be having this evening?" I asked as a distraction.

"We'll be dining on lemon pepper chicken breasts with braised Brussel sprouts, wine buttered linguine, and a tossed salad."

My mouth watered for more than the menu at this point.

"And buns," I added.

"Excuse me?" he asked as he blinked at me with a spatula in his hand.

My blush crept into a crimson mass while I fought to recover. What the hell was I doing? "I see you already have rolls on the table. What can I do to help you?" For the love of God, give me something to do so I don't have to talk.

"Would you mind pouring us some drinks?"

"Sure. What would you like?"

"There should be a nice white wine in the pantry, if you want to join me in a glass."

I turned my back on him and hoped he wasn't laughing at me. Feeling the draft by the pantry, I reminded myself to ask him about the passageway but the other things were swooped from my brain at the first glimpse of sexy bare toes by a steaming stove. The wine was there and had already been opened once, so it wasn't too difficult for me to remove the cork. He slipped crystal wine glasses from a cabinet and slid them to me across the countertop. After pouring him a generous amount, I only gave myself enough for a few sips. How worse could I get if I drank on top of already having the hormones of a teenage boy possess my body for the last hour or so?

Taking a sip in the silence that followed, I scanned everything he had accomplished for our non-date dinner. It was impressive.

"I hope this will be to your liking as I was stumped with what I should fix tonight."

"Dinner looks wonderful. You didn't have to go to all of this trouble," I stated softly.

"I don't get the chance to cook like this very often, so I got to flex my cooking muscles for an hour."

"You sound as if you used to cook quite a bit."

"After your grandmother passed away, Mr. Fenmore lost all inclination to eat, so I would cook for both of us."

His eyes were on the chicken he was plating, so I couldn't see any reaction in those lovely eyes of his. It touched me at how he had shown this type of emotion for such a gruff old miser.

"Let me say that your actions were appreciated. I wasn't told he was suffering in such a way, but it happens."

"He wasn't the type of man to tell all of his dirty laundry to family, even when they did ask. He suffered in silence until the old gardener killed Mrs. Fenmore's favorite rosebush."

A smile graced his face as he handed me a full plate of delicious smelling food. Keeping his plate and grabbing his less full glass of wine, he headed to the four-seater table in the breakfast area. I had seen the formal dining room but it looked far too old-fashioned for my lifestyle. It was beautiful but being raised on leftovers and simple meals, this formal room landed me way outside of my comfort zone.

Saying an internal prayer, I tried out the items carefully prepared for me. My taste buds were singing with each bite.

"My compliments to the chef. This is the best meal I've had in about a year."

Smiling at me, he ducked his head in thanks and scooped up his glass. "I would have guessed you had been on plenty of dates in such an amount of time. Did none of them take you anywhere outside of fast food or did you only meet up with guys at coffee shops?"

"Neither," I answered awkwardly.

He paused, waiting for more, but I didn't offer it. Peeking through my bangs, I saw the light change in his eyes as he went back to his meal.

"Okay. I think we need to get to know each other a little bit. But if anything makes you squeamish, it'll be considered off base for now. Sound fair?"

"Like just now?" I smiled at him and he returned the gesture. This was the most cordial smiling I had seen from him since showing up here.

"Agreed. But it has to be give and take, if not too personal a question."

"Agreed." He saluted me with his glass and I started wondering what would be discussed between the two of us. Just when I went to grab my drink, lightning crackled across the sky and I tipped my glass over onto the age loved linen.

"Oh. Oh my. I'll get it." I fumbled with my chair

and began to race for the towel at the stainless steel sink. By the time the dish towel was in my hand, he was already using both of our napkins to soak what there was of my spilled drink. Was I more embarrassed of the unknown dream of earlier or the glass of wine I gracefully knocked over in the middle of the small table? As I swept my hand in to join his, the touch of his skin meeting mine sent a jolt that had my body answering for me. The dream won my inner battle for blushing. His eyes met mine from under the fringe of his shaggy hair and my breath caught for about three seconds. Trying to untangle my cloth from his, he captured my fingers and held them as his eyes roved over my bent form. I could feel the weight of his gaze as it ran from my thighs pressed against the wood of the table to my eyes that rapidly blinked when his hunger absorbed into mine.

I gulped loudly and those eyes flicked to the warm spot on my flushed neck. The same spot he had caressed in my dream. His head tilted as if hearing the beat of my heart reach stampede levels. Lightning streaked across the skyline through the old windows in the kitchen and I felt my skin tingle with the amount of electricity running through the heavy air. Or was that from the touch of Kenrick's skin against mine? One of his fingers traced mine as the thunder boomed behind the flash of blinding light. The storm rolled closer and the room was already darkening enough to need additional light.

Using this as an excuse, I jumped away from him. "Since you've got that under control, we can throw it in the wash as we get the candles lit. We won't be able to appreciate the beauty of your cooking without them."

I walked off before he had a chance for a rebuttal and I heard him moving the dishes to the counter while I found the taper candles in the holders on the baker's rack by the pantry. The matches were right beside them so I struck one as another brilliant stream of light peeled around us. Once I had both candles lit and in my hands, I turned to help with the table, only to have Kenrick at my back and in my personal space. A cold breeze twirled about us from nowhere and I shivered, making the flames do a dance of shadows against the kitchen walls. Taking one from me, he walked through the cold air and back to the waiting table. He'd moved our meal in record time as I set my taper by my place setting that was back on the uncovered dining table.

Shivering from the lingering cool air, I ignored it as I went back to eating the remainder of my meal. After another shiver, he frowned.

"What?" I asked out of tense curiosity.

"It seems someone is walking over your grave and I do not like them getting your attention."

He had to be kidding me. Not only was it an odd way to phrase it but there was no way that he was jealous of anyone possibly being in my life. I ignored it and swallowed the last of my food. Still having a few bites left on his plate, I sipped at the wine he'd repoured for me as I waited to take his dish to the sink. Silence having been replaced by the sound of a light rain against the roof, I forced my shoulders to relax. This was going to turn into another vision and three was my limit for any given day. After the third, I tended to take a sleeping pill and make myself sleep the rest of the day away. Having already had two spells, I'd have to make up a good story on my passing out again.

Not having to wait long, he was done and pushing away from the table. I grasped the plates and rushed to the sink as I explained the cook didn't have to wash up. He chuckled and shrugged as I set the taps on for my task as the walls were sprayed with more flashes of light.

"Indulge an old man and leave the stainless steel sink alone while a storm is squabbling above our heads."

Giving a dubious look at his comment, I stuck my hand in the water but the loud roll of thunder made me jump away from the bubbles.

Touching my shoulder, he spoke louder. "Please? They won't mind waiting a few hours."

Giving him a shrug, I walked to my candlestick and turned back to him. "Where to now? Or is the dinner over?"

"Why would it be over? Have I done something to offend you?"

He actually sounded concerned, so I softened up.

"Everything is fine. Do we go into another room to talk or do you want to stay here?"

"Let's go into the front room and hang out on the sofa while we see how bad this storm is going to be. I'll grab the weather radio from the cabinet and join you there in a few minutes."

But as he was leaving the room, I could have sworn he mumbled, "Since you won't let me screw you senseless."

But he wouldn't say something so crass. Would he?

Chapter Ten

Not finding a comfortable spot to take up, especially after what I might have heard, I was just settling into the corner of the tapestry covered sofa when he came back in with a toaster-sized radio. I had left my glass of wine on the side table with the last few sips in it and had no intention of drinking more.

"As you probably have more questions than I do, you can go first." He settled in the blue high back chair closest to me.

Where to begin? I started with asking about what went on here on a daily basis and found it to be less stressful than I imagined but at a steady pace. They sold the pecans from that small grove, had part ownership in the wine being made at the property tied to our back lot, plus sold the items from the greenhouse at local markets. There were one florist and one produce man who got a third of the profits from any sold product. All of the proceeds were direct deposited into the property account and a stipend placed into a savings account for Kenrick's work. The sellers came to get the product, so it was less for me to have to do and Kenrick kept track of the weekly profit sheets from both vendors.

Finding this all fascinating, I felt a little more respect for the sullen businessman. He hadn't been living off of my grandfather as I had first thought but had been a helpful hand when health had taken a bit of time away from Mr. Fenmore. If I stayed, then we would see if Kenrick would be happy to keep on with his duties, for the same profit and lodging. That led me to another topic.

"I never see you coming or going but I'm guessing you have a room here," I asked already knowing the answer after my snoopfest earlier.

"You didn't see my room upstairs? I thought you'd been making yourself at home here."

Was I busted?

"I saw a more masculine room up on the third floor but didn't know if it belonged to you or not," I answered without meeting his steady gaze.

"Yes, the room by the attic space is mine and I'm pretty quiet in my actions as I've been on my own for a very long time."

I noticed the air had changed with those words, as if there was a lump of sadness heaved onto his statement.

"You're about my age, aren't you?"

"I'm an old soul, so it feels as if I've lived three different life spans," he said with a small chuckle.

"What type of education do you have?"

"Not much since I was raised on a farm many years ago. I've learned through grit and a tough life. I've only taken a few online courses and they were to help Mr. Fenmore with the accounting items that were more advanced than what he was used to from his earlier days. You aren't a college snob, are you?"

"Heavens, no. I went because I had to do something to better my life and it happens to be a career that I love on top of it all."

"Mr. Fenmore said you loved refurnishing vintage

items, right?"

"Yes, I took cabinetry, woodworking, and some business management classes at a technical college outside my hometown. The dorm was an old apartment building next door for the lower income students. I specialized in refurbishing old furniture and I'm thinking of doing it on the side if I stay here."

I waited to see how he would react. Not that I needed his permission.

"Sounds like a good way to pass the time, if it's what you want to do."

"I'm not the type of girl to lie about and wait for things to happen. I've got a tad more spunk, if you hadn't already noticed," I said with a bit more annoyance than intended but I didn't like his perception of what I'd do with my future here.

His hands came up. "No offense meant. Neither of us knows the other well enough to know how we'll handle the future."

I nodded and forced the acid out of my tongue as I had a retort ready to slip from my lips.

There was an awkward silence and then as we both began to speak at once, a slam resounded at the front door. Yelping, I jumped off the sofa but was too afraid to go to the door. Kenrick held up a hand and then proceeded to the door to look through the peephole.

"There's no one there," he stated before putting his hand on the knob.

He slipped it open slowly and what lay on the threshold was a plastic green pot that resembled the ones from the greenhouse. How the hell had it gotten there?

Frowning, he picked up the debris-covered pot and

held it in his hand as if it had popped there from sheer magic.

Finally, he spoke, "I guess I left the door open to the greenhouse because I have no clue as to why this would be here. Did you grab one for something earlier?"

After I shook my head, he carried the empty pot into the kitchen before he came back with the yellow raincoat I had glimpsed in the laundry area.

"I'm going to check on the door and will be right back, okay?"

He didn't even wait for an answer as he swooped into the wind that had picked up speed outside the thick walls. Picking up the glass, I went to rinse it out in the sink, but what happened was a bit more out of the normal for such a thing. Hearing a moan and a thump from outside the kitchen window, I was alarmed that maybe Kenrick had fallen down. Standing on tiptoe, I peered out the window to see if I could get a clear view but the rain poured too hard. I saw something but it was an outline. It didn't move as I stood there so I had to see if it was him and something had happened. Not having a raincoat for myself, I had to go out in the harsh weather unprotected.

Running at a speed of haste, I tried to make each step true on the slippery ground. I was soaked by the time I made it five yards from the front door. What I saw wasn't Kenrick but a woman. She stared at me from the middle of the yard. She was wearing a white sundress with a shawl over it. This specter had to be her but she was dead. Was I having another vision? Lightning struck in the trees above us and she pointed a long white arm to the greenhouse and then to the cemetery. What the fuck? I shook my head at her, more from disbelief than of misunderstanding. She repeated her gesture but her face became stern and furious. My gaze stayed locked on her as I tried to see what she wanted of me.

"I don't understand," I whispered more to myself in the midst of the thunder shaking the ground under me.

Her figure shook with rage and she flung her ghostly thin arms up to the sky before barreling at me on invisible legs. I ducked in defense as the frigid air of her spirit went through me and the light across the sky blinded me for a split second. I felt ill, like she'd yanked out my stomach when she'd traveled through my body. Wanting to heave, I took in great gulps of air before I slowly turned to see if she stood behind me like in some macabre nightmare. She wasn't. Kenrick was and his aura blazed for the piece of a second I had before another strike was thrown from the sky.

Blinking until my vision cleared again, Kenrick was in my face and yelling at me over the chaotic noise of the sky.

"What?" I couldn't make his words out but his stomping in the mud confirmed him being mad as hell at me. Had he seen her? Did he know what she wanted?

He struck out and grabbed my arm in a grip bordering on bruising in its strength. His tug almost had my knees in the wet ground, but his hold on me kept me up as well as racing back to the house with him.

Once he slammed the front door with his muddy boot, I turned my fury on him. "What the fuck is your problem?"

"Why were you out there? Are you insane?" he

raged.

"You wanna question my sanity when you were out there before me?"

"I was out there trying to check on the property, not to babysit you in a raging storm while you play tag with beacons of destruction."

"Why not say that I'm a witch praising the gods?"

His face stilled to chiseled marble. "Excuse me? What brought witches into this?"

I began to shake but it was more than the weather battling my emotions. It was as if our inner turmoil had become part of the storm itself.

He took a step closer, seeming to grow in size as he menacingly loomed over my trembling form. "Answer me!"

Slipping back a step, my wet socks had no purchase on the foyer floor. I yelped as I began to fall but yipped in surprise as his arms caught me before I hit the slick floor.

"Do you have to keep touching me?" I asked with too much irritation as he was only trying to help me.

"Yes, as a matter of fact, I do," was his unexpected response. I blinked at him as I fought for the proper words or retort.

"If you insist on needing me, then I will insist on taking care of you." The flash in the sky was mirrored in the eyes that were entirely too close to mine. Was he going to kiss me for real and would it compare to the heated ones from my dreams? Just as he moved in and my lips parted of their own will, the front door flew open and smacked him in the back, making him almost dropping me in the process. Getting the much-needed interruption, I scooted away and started taking off the wet wool that had me in this situation. He slammed the door shut and latched it as I balled up the wet socks in my hands.

"You'd best get into something warmer as I won't be the cause of you leaving with pneumonia." He gave one last look at the door and walked back toward the laundry room, leaving me to speculate as to what he meant.

After a moment, I shivered again and shrugged before I forced myself to trek back up to my room and the clothes which had been left for me from the enigma which had me blushing. Not wanting to appear anymore enamored of him, I threw on the sweat suit I had and it would douse any flames he thought I was harboring as it was a faded forest green that was thin in a few places and extremely baggy in others. I had to use the less thick socks and was grumpy at the moisture in the air keeping my shoes from being dry. I would just feel better if I went down there in a complete outfit this time.

Careful to not slip down the lacquered steps, I headed to the kitchen to see if Kenrick was still back there. He wasn't lounging in the front room and I hadn't heard him go upstairs, so he had to be around here somewhere. Feeling foolish, I poured myself a glass of water as I waited for him to reappear. I downed the first glass and began another one when I felt something behind me. Turning slowly, I saw Kenrick coming through the dim lit door by the pantry. He started when he saw me standing silently by the sink. Shutting the door and avoiding eye contact, he hung the raincoat on the hook in the laundry area and stood by the breakfast table, waiting. So, I did what was expected of me.

"I've been meaning to ask you what was down that hallway. It seems creepy and seldom used but I can feel a draft coming from it."

It softly stated how I hadn't been nosey enough to see what lay at the end of the narrow path but I wasn't going to allow him to ignore where he had popped in from.

"It's the emergency exit from the house. It was originally the servant's entrance but your grandmother was against such prejudices, so it remained as a way to escape in case of a fire or if being robbed. It made Mr. Fenmore feel more secure if she always had a way to safety."

"That doesn't answer what you were doing."

"You didn't ask."

Sighing, I fought my quick temper with him since I didn't want a blooming fight on my hands after so many visions had crippled my emotions.

"I thought we had a truce?" I asked softly.

"We do but that doesn't mean you have a license to be bossy and a busybody."

"Excuse me but I thought the reason I was here was to possibly take over the property, so my question is valid. Are you going to cause me problems if I accept my stepgrandfather's offer and work the property?" I set my glass down and stalked over to the table, keeping its sturdiness between us.

"You want honesty? You've got it. No, I don't want you here but it wasn't my decision to make. I'm the one who picked up the pieces when your grandmother passed away and the business slid to practically no income going to fund Mr. Fenmore's needs. I held his hand as he cried over the loss of the woman he loved while you were in your own little world. He wasn't even your blood and you act like this place already belongs to you. How long has it been since you even stepped your dainty little toes onto the property?"

I bounded around the table and got in his face by the time I registered his eyes going molten. Not letting him back me down, I stepped right into the fight at hand. It was going to be as harsh as the rain pounding at the roof. I had to raise my voice to be heard over the sky yelling back at us.

"You speak of blood but you aren't even close enough to claiming this place for your own. You worked it at the permission of a frail man who needed help. You moved yourself into this home and made yourself lord and master as you saw him slowly die. You have no ground to claim in this matter."

Inwardly, I winced as my words hit him like a slap across his aristocratically handsome face. His nostrils flared and streaks of anger lit the room from the beating going on outside. The windows creaked at the onslaught against their frail looking exterior. I knew that feeling. I had embraced it my whole life as I had been placed as everyone's second thought. I had fought for the few things I owned and this stranger was not going to take away a future that may brighten my meager existence.

"I didn't ask for this to happen to me and I know the same is of you. We're both part of the next step. You didn't ask for some chick to waltz in here thinking she deserved the world on a platter and I didn't expect an arrogant man to be here to tell me I had lived my life the wrong way. This is no more my fault than my visions of witches and their stupid books of secrets and embellished stories. But I'm no misplaced child so don't treat me like I need to be raised. I'm here. You're here. We need to come to an agreement or you need to leave."

By this time, I was inches away and seething in my own stew. The cat was out of the bag on my level of abnormality. I needed to say my piece and walk away before I tossed myself into a vision that would have him knowing just how vulnerable I was during high emotions. I'd had it happen a few times and those individuals knew how to work me to the point where I became a mass of nerves and anxiety medications. Not this time. I had a will of my own to back the one that had brought me here.

"Witch?" was all he asked as I calmed down enough to make out the narrowing of his eyes. He was afraid. The tension left the room like an unwanted guest.

"I have visions. Okay? I'm aware that I'm a freak of nature and you've already been witness to my little episodes, so don't act surprised."

"You let me believe you were a woman prone to fainting? Well, it explains some things but what does a witch and her diary have to do with it?"

"Who said it was a diary?" Stepping away from him, I caught his mistake.

"Fuck!" he muttered with a hoarse curse as he knew he'd been busted.

"What do you know of this woman? Why is she visiting me, and what the hell is so scary about her diary that you don't want me knowing about it?"

As if he'd be honest now. Right.

"Nothing. It's just an old wives' tale told to me the first time I came here and didn't think I'd ever hear about it again."

"Tell me the story. I'm curious as to whether it even comes close to the visions I've been having."

I found it strange how calmly he absorbed the fact I was a type of psychic. Nobody took it very well, not even my grandmother the first time I had gotten one in front of her. After that, and a bunch of research, we took it in stride and looked for the signs of when they would come on. She kept a diary of the days she witnessed me having them and each one of them was a rough day in my preadolescent years. I don't think I would have survived high school if it hadn't been for that tidbit.

"Someone made up a story to spook the natives, so what's the point in wasting time on it?"

"Indulge me. If nothing else, it's worth a laugh. And you were the one to say the evening wasn't over yet unless you want to end it here?"

A siren came over the forgotten radio with a warning from the weather service stating extreme amounts of waterfall and the area would be at flood levels in the next hour as it circled. We were in here for the night and suddenly the stress of it wrapped around me like an unwanted hug. Something had changed and I prayed it was just the electricity in the air ripe with strain.

My heart beat like a cardiac patient having a stress test. My hand was on my chest and it distracted his glance from the disturbing news spewing from the radio in tandem.

"Are you all right?"

Now he asked. I giggled and it grew into a fit of laughter as his face grew sour with my humor in the situation. It wasn't funny but I couldn't stop laughing. Actually, if I hadn't let it go then I would have been in for a worse night than the weatherman could ever predict.

Choking down some of it, I said, "I'm sorry but I needed that."

Blinking at me, he still didn't get it but I was okay with not being understood. Being who I was, I never believed anyone would ever understand what went on in my head.

"From what the radio is blaring, we'll be stuck here listening for further alerts for the next hour. Unless you have something better to do, we have conversations to finish. We'll start with the ghost story and then go back to what we were discussing before our tromp in the rain."

Eyeing him, I dared him to walk away or say there was nothing further to discuss. The ball was in his court to prove to me we could be decent to each other in a normal situation, if anything in my life would ever be considered as normal.

Kenrick eyed me suspiciously but nodded.

"Where to?" I was willing to let him even pick the setting.

"Our library," he said as he smiled down at me.

That killed my laughter faster than anything ever had in my life.

Chapter Eleven

After I avoided the gold high back from before, I sat in the sleek desk chair. My shrink would have said I had to put myself in the dominant role but I just couldn't look at Kenrick while sitting in that spot. I was fighting the flush on my cheeks from just recalling the heat of the kiss I had gotten while seated there.

"You can ask me one question before I stare at you until you spill the beans, mister."

"Seriously?"

"Yes, and there went your one question," I teased.

Glaring at him over the wood of the desk, I waited. Refusing to break eye contact, I didn't even move. After a moment, he shifted in his seat. I smiled at him while remaining still. The feeling of accomplishment washed over me as I had him in a corner.

"Fine," he spat out and I leaned back to get more comfortable.

Moving the candlestick over, I watched him as he fidgeted with the radio.

"The secret hallway was settled, right?" he asked as he kept looking away from me.

"Yes, that's been explained. You can get back on one of the other topics or I can start my list of questions for you. Your choice."

"Starting it off on a better note, I'm not mad about you being here. What I'm concerned about is my life changing. I don't like change unless I know for certain it's for the better. You being here will unsettle things and I'm not sure I can accept the upheaval."

"So, you're more concerned about the changes I will make instead of me being the one making them?" I was confused because if I were in his shoes my first issue would be someone kicking me out.

"Correct. My gut tells me you aren't mean-tempered enough to fight for me to be booted from the home I've had for a few years, especially as I kept it going when Mr. Fenmore became ill and like yourself, I have nowhere else to go."

I felt better about his opinion of me but fought the smile that edged my lips.

"You're right. I would only do that if I saw no other way for us to co-exist here."

"Then I'm glad I was right about something. How do you feel about me being here?'

"I believe you did what you could to protect the estate and would like to keep it going since you obviously have the experience to see this place prosper."

"That's not what I asked"—he smiled at me—"but I'll take it for now."

Oh boy. I was not about to tell him I found him sexy but creepy in the same respect. Or my mind-blowing imaginary sex with him. I thanked God I hadn't kept drinking the wine.

"We settled another topic. Good," I proclaimed as to push aside my inner thoughts.

"What expectations do you have here?" he asked me.

"Great question." And not of a personal nature. "I

want things to be the same as they have been with the deals regarding produce, nuts, and plants. The winery is a contract I will have to learn better, but it's set in stone for a few more years. As you have the complete knowledge of the minute details, I would ask if you wanted to continue as things were before my step-grandfather passed away. The only difference there is I would be the one you reported to and I would have the final say on any changes for the future. You would be able to remain living here, as long as we could live under the same roof with a comfortable outcome."

He chuckled. "I've never heard roommates put in such a manner before. It must be from your college experiences."

I nodded as I had dealt with clutter laden divas in the dorm rooms, not a sullen lean man I was attracted to.

"We'll try to get to know each other and respect each other's space, right?" he asked and my mind flicked over me sneaking into his bedroom. Had he known I had done that? If not, I wasn't about to blab now. Instead, I put my hand out and came around the desk to him.

He stood up and looked down at my offered hand. A moment of contemplation passed by and I looked down to see if there was something on my hand to keep him from shaking it. There wasn't, of course, so I glanced back up and saw his eyes flicker before he moved quickly to hold mine. A tingle went up my arm and my mouth formed an "O" before I took in him smirking at me. Then he used his grip on my hand to pull me closer. It all happened so fast I barely grabbed onto his shirt before my body hit the front of his.

"I'm an old Cajun boy. Let me make this official." He pressed a gentle kiss to my slightly parted lips.

Those lips felt the same as they had in my dreams, heavenly and sinful. He didn't make any further advance but wasn't moving away from me either. Was he waiting for me to kiss him back? My mind, and my libido, screamed at once but with different answers. Backing away slowly, I was sad I couldn't ravage him here and now but that was not going to happen. I was wide awake and this man was very real.

Instead of going back behind the desk to hide, I forced myself to sit in the high back chair opposite his, far enough away to make me feel better. Settling in with my legs to my chin, I tried to hide the blush creeping up my neck. Hopefully, it was dark enough to keep it hidden from him.

"Now, what about this ghost story you're avoiding?"

"Go ahead and change the subject. That's fine, even if it doesn't have anything to do with the deal we just made. And I'm not avoiding it, I just think our evening could be more fun if we didn't waste it on silly tales from eons ago."

Knowing I was too chicken to take his bait, I kept to my course. "Tell the story and I'll decide whether it's a waste of breath or not." I smiled to see if it helped because I really did want to hear what he'd been told. Maybe it was his reaction to my mentioning her that had my radar picking up his need to drop the subject but something metaphysical was going on here.

"Fine. Geez. A long time ago, a family lived in an estate near here and they did the same type of business as Mr. Fenmore. That's why I was told the tale of the

Witch's Love Diary."

He paused and I waved him onward. He gave me an exasperated look but continued.

"The daughter of the house was being educated by a nanny half of the day and she worked on the property the other half of it. They had a greenhouse full of herbs and plants specifically grown for the holistic community. Grapes were grown for a local winery and marketers would come to the property to purchase items for themselves or to sell at the market. The daughter was a wonder at the holistic items and kept a log of what she grew and how to maximize the growth as she received a profit when the seasons were plentiful. Her mother had passed away when she was small so she took great comfort in doing what her mother had loved and her father had been glad to have her out from under his feet when he was selling the items off.

The abnormal thing about this was her interest in the plants being more than just for profit as she was rumored to be making potions out of them. Girls in the area whispered the young lady had fallen for one of the farmers and was attempting to make a potion so he would fall in love with her and take her away from the town. People said she started using her ledger book as a spell book and then when she ran out of room, she bought a leather-bound diary to keep her information hidden in. Supposedly, she used the profit money to buy the book as her father believed it was better to use it on new clothing or shoes. But they say that wasn't her interest and buying it would annoy her father, so she purchased it. It was to be her first step in being her own person, which was not what her father had planned for her."

"Sounds fascinating. Do you know if she ever got the man of her dreams?"

"Funny you worded it that way."

"Why?" I asked.

"The tale goes that she did finish the love spell and had let a few girls try it out before she attempted to use it on her intended. They stated the girls were successful in obtaining the loves of their chosen men, so she took the final step to use it on her unsuspecting farmer. She set out to seduce him one night, and if he didn't fall into her arms, she would make sure the spell took care of the rest. Her pride had her trying the seduction first, thinking it was going to go perfectly either way. She had no idea it would end up so badly."

"Oh no, he turned her down? Or did the potion not work on him?"

"You have this figured out, don't you? I don't even need to tell you the rest."

"No, tell me the rest!" I appealed while I sat on the edge of my chair.

"She did get him to come to the greenhouse one night, as she had told him the plants were the beginnings of her next batch to sell. They say he was half into the seduction when she dropped the vial of potion onto the ground while fumbling with her clothes. He saw it and became so appalled at her that he called her a witch and told her he'd never marry a woman who would use the earth to manipulate people. She was outraged and said his fate would be sealed with hers and began to laugh at him for thinking he was strong enough to evade her wishes. He somehow got the courage to leave the greenhouse, after smashing her glass vial into the greenhouse floor, and ran away into the rainy night."

"He's lucky she didn't douse him with it." I slid back into my seat.

"Well, that's not the end of the tale," he baited.

He paused so I waited for him to finish the story. He drank down his glass of wine and looked back at me with a mischievous grin.

"He was said to be found the very next morning, lying in the cemetery, with a raging fever while experiencing bouts of delirium. The town folk thought he got a chill from the cold and rainy night. After a long month of being sickly, he got an unsuspected visitor. The witch was back and she said to him that she had cursed him for his follies. If she couldn't have his love then he couldn't have any real love of his own. He was doomed to never know true love anywhere other than his dreams, where he would burn in a never-ending fever. She would burn for him the rest of her days and he would pay the same price."

"Holy crap!"

"There was nothing holy about it. He was cursed and then shunned, even when the young lady disappeared from the town. She never returned and they wonder if she took his soul with her into the night."

Thunder roared and I squealed.

A gust of laughter came out of him at my shock. "It's just a story, Renata."

The look in his eyes didn't match the mockery on his face. Her story had scared him, even if from a time long ago. Some things could haunt you for a lifetime, real or imaginary, and this was one of those things.

"Now, I think we should retire for the evening," he said as he stood to stretch slowly. The black cotton came up to show me a glimpse of defined stomach that was a dream to touch. I wanted to run my fingernails over it to see if it was indeed the same pleasure. Somehow, I knew it would be even better but I wasn't about to assault him to find out.

Picking up my candlestick and my glass, I headed back to my room with Kenrick trailing behind me. As I stopped in front of my closed door, I turned to see if he would walk on to his own space. Surprised at how close he stood to me, I reached for the doorknob behind my rod-straight back, but the glass clanked against the hard wood. He had a Mona Lisa smile on his face as he leaned down to me. Inching away, my back met the stained wood as I held my breath. Just a trace of cool air was between us as he hung above my waiting lips. Then just as quickly, he kissed me with enough pressure to almost bang my head but was gone by the time it made contact.

Dazedly going into my room, I went to sit on my bed, forgetting not only did I not put the candle and glass down but I still had a pile of clothes waiting to be put up. Laughing at myself, I set about handling all of this so I could crawl into bed and relax. If I was lucky, the storm wouldn't keep me up and I'd sleep a little later in the morning. But we know my luck wasn't the best so I'd be happy with getting a decent six hours before I had to go make myself some strong coffee. I knew my visions had me a bit more mentally worn but I was in good enough shape to get through it while not letting myself think over anything else today. My mind needed a break and I was going to meditate until I could shut everything down.

The beat of the weather outside seemed to be at a

slower pace so we were out of any trouble. The tempo was mellow compared to the raging measure of earlier. Soothing me in its tapping against the windows, I got into my nightshirt before I slipped under the cool covers of my bed. The only other thought I allowed myself was that I expected to see Mr. White tomorrow. Sighing, I wrapped my mind in a blanket of silken protection as I welcomed the dark to pull me under its refreshing spell. This was one of the only true friends I had and her name was Oblivion. Like most friends, she could be fickle and tonight had become one of those nights.

Having to keep your mind a blank slate while tossing and turning is a tough job but I'd accomplished it before. Finally finding a more comfortable position, my mind wandered to small scenes from today and I knew I should stop the mental barrage. All of the pictures flashed before me like an amateur slideshow as my mind absorbed so many small details. Until one of the pictures stopped and it was of me looking out at the greenhouse. Looking down, I saw my legs below me and not the white dress of Aster, so that meant I had begun to fall asleep and this wasn't going to be too awful.

There was a pull of energy coming from the greenhouse, so I let it take me to where I was meant to be in this little scene. The back of a young lady stood in front of me and she was busy attending to a row of plants. Her long chestnut hair had been woven in a tight braid going down her graceful back. Tiptoeing closer, I waited for her to turn to me. Was I in a vision of her previous life or was my sleeping mind trying to work through the story Kenrick had told me? There seemed to be only one way to find out and even that wasn't cut and dry.

Peering around her, I saw she was using a pair of old sheers to cut leaves off of several small plants in front of her. They were all in a neat row and isolated from the others as if they were a new project or being safeguarded for some reason. Wondering if these were the ones from the tale, I looked over her other shoulder to see the leather-bound book from the attic. She had it open toward the middle as she had surpassed it being a simple diary and was using it to make spell notations. There were diagrams of plant leaves and measurements below them. Above the sketches was one simple French word, Aimer, which meant love. This had to be her recipe for the love potion.

She was singing songs in French as she clipped the items on her list and set them in different places on a large handmade ceramic platter. Then she started talking to herself.

"Oh sweet love, you think you can pass me by. You are such a silly man. Those strong arms are meant to be around me and only me. As you don't have a current lover, this is the perfect time to make you see me as you should. If this batch works, then we'll both be happy and in love."

She went back to her French lyrics of passion and undying love and somehow I could understand them. I'd taken the basics of French in high school but it was as if I had internal subtitles in my head as to what she sang. It was creepy and yet poignant.

Then a voice began calling Aster's name. It had to be her father wondering where she was. She returned his call, stating she would be there in a moment. She hurriedly covered the platter with a linen cloth and slipped the scissors into the pocket of the white apron she wore over her simple dress. The platter was slipped under the tray of plants and then covered by a piece of burlap as to hide it from any quick once over by anyone who came in. Dusting her hands off on her apron, she took a look over her shoulder and walked through me as if I wasn't even there and went out of the greenhouse humming her French song.

The problem was she had left her book on the shelf with her plants and it seemed odd to me. Why would she hide the plants but not her book? Looking closely at the book, I made out more of the recipe she had written down. The plants were exotic and must be why she had just a handful of stems coming from the new buds. They weren't labeled so she had to have them memorized but the drawings helped me to pick out what each one was. The potion had to be set aside for two nights, in a dark place, as it became more potent. It had a short lifespan so it had to be ingested by the fourth night after being mixed. That meant she intended to use it this week on her crush. Then I heard footsteps and fought the need to hide. It was a dream so no one would see me here anyway.

As I went to turn toward the door, Aster came running in, breezing through me again. It gave me a chill at the feeling of her slipping into me like I was fog. She had a smile as she got to the book and closed it. There was a shelf way above her tray of plants and she hefted the leather up onto it, pushing it back out of view as she hopped up a few times. It was properly hidden now and she giggled in satisfaction at her plan, bringing glee to her actions. Her confidence was a glow about her as she knew she would have her man before the next harvest. The seduction was planned and she'd be able to take her love from here as they started a new life in a different town, away from the father that thought he knew the best for her. She wouldn't marry the neighbor her father had mentioned and she wasn't going to stay here and be made to tend two farms for the rest of her life. She wanted passion, her potions, and to travel the world as she found a home where she could raise babies along with her power as a witch.

She turned on her toes and looked through me as if I was glass. But then her eyes narrowed and she smiled so brightly it was alarming. I turned to see who stood behind me but no one was standing there. Gazing back at her, she had stepped closer to me. I backed up a step and she laughed. Holy shit, she was looking at me. She nodded and pointed at the book that was out of sight then pointed back at me.

"What?" I asked her.

She laughed again and this time it held a frigid edge to it. It ran along my body as if charged with electricity. Aster took a step closer and I found myself unable to move away from her. Her pale arm reached out and she let her fingertips glance over my neck and down to where my heart pounded against my sleeping chest. I had to remind myself that I wasn't even here. I was in bed letting my mind wander over the ghost story that had wrapped around me before I had meditated. I should have blanked my mind out better as this might not have happened if I had.

"You simple woman, you think I didn't know you were here? I left the book for you to look over. How far did you get, my dear?"

"I saw the potion but nothing more," I replied, terrified this was turning into such a nightmare. One that I wasn't successful in waking myself from.

Her palm lay flat against my breastbone and a tingle ran into it as she closed her eyes and hummed. My breath was stolen from me as the tingle became so strong that a buzz rang in my ears. She pushed her nails into my thin skin, and I bit back a yelp as a burn set into my lungs.

"Such a strong woman. I have made an excellent choice. Not only are you beautiful but gifted as well. You're not as powerful as I had hoped but with my gifts, you can be a woman to change time itself. I can feel it in your heart. You have learned to fight for your beliefs and where you belong. Maybe I should stay here and not run off after the ceremony. Your fresh mind has given me possibilities not available to me one hundred years ago. This is an intriguing turn of events."

Wheezing out the words, I asked, "What are you talking about?"

Her laugh went from her chest and into mine like a turning of a knife. "You and I are about to be as close as twin sisters, my dear. Just you wait and see." And with that, her nails went into the layers of my muscle and dug in between my ribs. It was as if her nails were sizzling while they punctured my lungs and tickled at my vulnerable heart. Pain so sharp it cut every nerve in my body and had me feeling as if I was a marionette whose master had cut her strings to fall apart on the stage floor. I screamed and oblivion of an evil nature took me in its arms and cradled me as I gasped my last sleeping breath.

Chapter Twelve

The stroke of a match caught my attention in the dark of my room. I opened my eyes to see the silhouette of the person holding the relit candle. It was Kenrick and he had knocked me out of the nightmare that had me in its clutches. Taking a few steadying breaths, I watched as he set the candle holder on the table at my bedside and bent over me.

"Are you all right, Renata?"

"Yes, did I wake you?"

I felt uncomfortable about him being in my room but if he hadn't shown up there was no telling how bad the dream would have gotten.

"No, I had planned on staying up to listen to the weather reports and heard you down the hall," he answered as he sat on the foot of the bed at my feet.

"I'm sorry to have disturbed you," I said in a light voice.

"It's not a problem. I thought I heard something and came down to you shaking the bed frame. Was it that bad of a dream?"

"It was getting there quickly and I'm embarrassed you heard me."

"You weren't making sex noises, so it's no big deal."

"Oh God!" I moaned as I hid my face in one of the pillows.

"Well, *now* you did." He burst out laughing.

Just great. I wake up from a nightmare to have a sexy man laughing at me in my own bedroom. This was just great for my self-confidence.

"You can go back to your room now. I can't have you being a bear tomorrow on my account," I said in a slightly dismissive tone.

"If I'm grumpy then it'll be my own fault and not yours. I'm the one too paranoid to sleep and you're the one trying to catch up on some, so it would seem."

"You don't even know me and you can instantly grasp that I'm tired?"

This just kept getting better and better.

"You've taken a few naps while you've been here and from what I've learned of your life, it was too busy to be spent catnapping. Am I right?"

"Yes, you are, but you aren't supposed to know me so well. We weren't even really on speaking terms until the truce, so neither one of us had really had the time to share any sordid stories."

"Mrs. Fenmore would talk about you after getting one of the letters you sent from college. She would share a few memories with me after reading each one of them.

She missed you but was so proud that you were doing what made you happy."

"She's the one who convinced me to go in the first place."

"You had her adoration, and I was envious of you."

"I'm sure you had loved ones. Who doesn't?"

"I was tossed out at a very young age for being a rebel and then got lucky enough to find a man who let me take care of his property. Other than that, I've had no long-term girlfriends or drinking buddies."

"No serious girlfriends? I find it hard to believe," I stated while I propped myself up on my pillows. There was no lying back down until he decided to leave my room.

"Why is that such a surprise to you?" he asked.

"Seriously? Come on?"

"I'm dead serious."

"Well, you're handsome, talented, and a hard worker. If you didn't possess the last two qualities then my grandfather wouldn't have hired you on."

"You think I'm handsome?"

"Oh geez! Are we really going to have this discussion?"

"Why is it a difficult topic? You brought it up," he reminded me.

"Fine. You are what most would consider to have sexy nerd qualities that are adorable and charming at the same time. Well, when you're being nice."

A chuckle rumbled in his chest, and he didn't stop it from curling in the air around us. It was good to hear him laugh. He needed to do it more often, and I told him so.

"I'd like to add that I can be very nice when properly motivated." He sighed and batted his eyelashes before going on. "So far we have established that sex noises are embarrassing, I'm nerdy sexy, and I need to laugh more. Anything else?"

Lord, what could I possibly say? Yes, Kenrick, in my dreams you fuck like a pro. *Oh my goodness, no!* I'd die before the words hit the atmosphere. Death by embarrassment. My head would explode from the abundant blood rushing to it from every part of my body.

"Why are you turning a nice shade of pink?"

"This whole conversation is ludicrous." I fidgeted with the blankets wrapped around my torso.

"I like the way you blush but you typically don't unless it's sexual in nature. Am I right?"

"I'm not even going there. We both need to go to bed and get some rest." I tried not to look him in those lovely eyes.

"We need to go to bed?" he asked with a gleam of mischief about him.

"Yes, we do." And then it hit me how I sounded. By the time my blush deepened and my face heated, he was kissing me.

Against my mouth, he whispered, "Best. Idea. All. Day." Then he started kissing me so deeply there were no words in my brain.

I matched his passion and grabbed at him. He made the first pass at me when we were talking earlier this evening, and now he had invited himself into my room. This kiss was meant to start a fire and I was the kindling just waiting for his blaze. He tasted so good. It was even better than the ones I had dreamed of. And to think this was the real life Kenrick in my bed, not the figment of my imagination. Butterflies flew in my stomach as his tongue swept across mine like warm velvet. I was practically panting for more, and we were both totally dressed.

He slipped across the bed and settled himself above me while I leaned against the pillows piled against the headboard. It was so intimate having him see the expressions on my face. If we'd been making love in this position then I would have been more vulnerable than in any conversation we could possibly have. This was eye to eye and breath to breath. Suddenly, I wished I'd worn something more attractive than a thin nightshirt but at least it wasn't a cartoon character shirt.

He played with the wisps of my hair spread against the cotton pillow cover. I wanted him to bury his fingers in the strands and pull me into him, to be conquered and left completely ravaged. I'd never felt this way before and it put the dream to shame. Running my hands over his shoulders felt wonderful and he slid up in a way where the muscle rolled under his skin. It was the image of a lion with the ability to pounce on its prey at any given moment. And this cat could devour me at any time.

I shivered as he slid his sinful mouth over my chin and down to nip at my collarbone. My nails dug into the masculine expanse of his shoulder blades and I gasped as he hit a spot that had my core heating up. Just a kiss and I became instantly ready for him to thrust into me. Was I a slut or had the dreams reminded my body of what it had been missing for so long? I wanted him and we were both consenting adults. I pulled him up for another kiss and hoped I was giving as good as I had gotten. A moan sounded from him and it drove me onward. My hands were sliding up the back of his t-shirt when a loud noise had us both jumping.

It was the window by my headboard, something had hit it.

"Must be the storm," Kenrick said as he paused to see if it would happen again.

"Probably," I stuttered and waited for him to either kiss me or move away from the bed.

After a moment, nothing else happened except the

tinkling of the rain against the window pane.

"Where was I? Ah, right here," he said as he nipped my other collarbone.

Just as I gasped at the pleasure, the window shattered all over the room.

Wind came whirling into the room as if a tiny tornado had been set loose on us. It whipped the glass to nick at our skin and had us both jumping for cover. I was on the opposite side of the bed with the cover pulled over me but I had to stay away from the fragmented glass spread across the floor. The wind screamed at us from the bedside, and I was afraid to look as the glass would rip my face to shreds.

"What the hell happened? Are we in the middle of a tornado?" I yelled at Kenrick who hid in the covers with me.

I was amazed at how quickly we had jumped off of the mattress. Adrenaline beat out the passion fading from my veins, and I clutched at him.

"No, we were in the clear," came his muffled response.

"Please tell me I'm asleep and this is still my nightmare. Please?"

"If it is a dream then we're both having the same one because I am most certainly here," he yelled above the wail of wind.

I listened carefully and the wind resembled a wailing spirit. It was eerie how human it sounded. Wind didn't do this. My spine crawled with the energy that swept around us. Something told me to see what was going on. My senses were itching with what was taking place.

Grabbing a handful of the cover, I peeked out the

corner closest to the head of the bed.

"Don't do it, Renata," yelled Kenrick as he tried to pull the blanket back around us. I felt the pings of glass bounce against our protection.

Prying it away from him, I saw what he didn't want me to see. Aster's form hovered above the bed as she wordlessly screamed at us. *What the hell?* She came barreling down on me, and I scrambled to move away from the bed. I didn't want to be pinned against the frame with glass to one side and her on the other. I had to get out of the room. The door remained ajar and if I moved fast enough I could avoid her. Just as I scampered out of the covers, ignoring Kenrick bellowing for me, I slipped and hit the dangerous shard covered floor under me. Cuts were the last thing on my mind as I saw her face twist in a mocking smile that chilled me to the bone.

****

Waking up in the attic was not what I had expected. Neither was the ghost singing as she moved around my prone figure. Her white summer dress floated around her ethereal figure and the hem skated over my legs, making me shiver. Pretending to still be unconscious, I perused the room from under my eyelashes. Apparitions being unable to hold matter was now marked as a myth in my shell-shocked world. Aster was gliding around, collecting items and setting them on the trunk which held her diary. Opposite of me sat Kenrick, who had been tied to an antique chair that he was bent over. I could see his chest moving as it took in oxygen but his face wasn't visible through the curtain of his hair. I hoped he was pretending to be out cold instead of actually being seriously injured. It made me wonder what a ghost like her could do to us and it frightened me that we were about to find out.

The storm still roared as it echoed through the wood rafters. Aster giggled with glee as she set up several candles across the leather trunk. Her diary laid open in the middle of them and the flickering flames of the light held the pages in an eerie glow. She had the sheers from my vision in her apron pocket and I saw her bending over a large platter that held a ceramic bowl. I recognized the plate and all of this did not bode well. She was material enough that the air stirred around her movements but I could still see a shadow of the objects behind her. Spooky. Was she physical enough to be injured? Had she already performed a spell on us? Were we too late to stop her?

"Renata, you can stop the pretense now. I knew the moment you mentally woke to us," came a high pitch voice which was more melodious than the one I had in my vision.

It was perky and childlike yet with a mature tone that showed age in its word choices. I bet many had mistaken her voice for the innocence of a young girl but few knew the evil temptress within.

"What's going on?" was my first silly question.

"As you are gifted, but not as a witch, I don't mind sharing my actions with you. I'm preparing my things for a special spell. You will be one subject and my dear love will be the other," she stated simply as she moved her fingers into the contents of the bowl. There was powder coating her fingertips and she added several bits of green from the platter on the floor.

If there was no sense acting like I was asleep then I might as well start checking out what she was up to.

First, I would have to see how many needed to be saved here.

"Is Kenrick out cold?" I asked her.

"I slammed your bed on top of him, but he should come to shortly. He's no good to me if he's dead."

I prayed she was correct because I had fallen for him. Damn it. How had I allowed it to happen? I barely knew him but the thought of him being hurt by this psycho made my heart stop mid-beat. If we got ourselves out of this, I was going to see if we could make this work. But how did I get us safely away from a ghost who had us tucked away in the attic?

"Do you mind if I ask what your plans are?"

I sat up and crossed my ankles, noticing there were several streams of blood coming from different sized cuts on my legs and feet. I remembered being on my knees when we dove off of my bed and looked to see what was tearing up the room, but not how I had cut up the top of my feet.

"Would you rather ask me about your injuries?" she asked as she glanced at me from the corner of her eyes. She had stopped in her actions as I had taken notice of my oozing wounds.

A few of them had already scabbed over but the larger ones were reopened by my actions. Why couldn't I recall what had happened? It bothered me almost as much as my feelings for Kenrick.

"Yes, please tell me what caused this?" I fought to keep my voice calm and polite as I knew it would get me better results than arrogance or hysteria.

"You reached out to me but the force of my power knocked you away from Kenrick and across the floor. You were senseless at that point and Kenrick jumped up to save you. It was his own undoing, and I wasn't going to allow it to happen. I toppled the bed frame over and the headboard hit him in the back of the head just as he was about to grab you."

"Why do you need us to be separated?"

"You two lovers can be together once I finish my plans for this evening."

"I'm confused. Can you elaborate?"

"Of course, my dear. You see, I've had my eyes on Mr. Giles for many years and after this evening, I'll have a second chance with him. It's one of the things I didn't get to accomplish before I died, and it makes me very sad."

She was looney. Even when I'd been in the hospital, I hadn't run across someone like her. She was all innocent and light but with a severe god complex. She could no more twist the hands of fate than she could the sands of time.

Then it hit me. No. No way. I couldn't be right. There was no way he could be the one. I looked at her and she gave me her full attention. Her eyes flickered as she took in the look of astonishment on my stunned face.

"Yes. Kenrick Giles was the man I had set out to marry. Why else do you think that I'm so interested in his well-being?"

"There's no way he's the man from your book. He's about my age so it had to be his father or grandfather."

"And you think a simple little witch like myself couldn't have something to do with that small detail?"

It couldn't be true. How could she make him live this long unless she'd cast a much more powerful spell than the one she was attempting now.

She walked over to Kenrick and lifted his face up by his mussed locks. His eyes opened and fear spread through them as he took in where he was.

"What have you done?" he asked in a trembling voice.

"Nothing. Yet."

Yanking her hand away, his head snapped back with the force of her sudden release of him.

"We girls were just speaking of your timeless good looks," she said with a large amount of glee.

"Renata, are you okay?" he asked me.

"I'm fine, even if I don't remember how I got here or what happened to cause my injuries. How are you?"

"I have a headache the size of this house and I know exactly what caused it," he stated as he sent a withering look over to Aster's book as she had turned back to reread a passage.

"I was naughty to my poor Kenrick. Wasn't I, my dear Cajun?"

"Obviously, you wanted my undivided attention, Aster. Well, now you've got it. What do you want?"

"The same thing that I wanted before, *you.*"

Chapter Thirteen

"I didn't love you then and certainly don't love you now, witch," he spat that as if it was the foulest of words he'd ever uttered.

"Tsk tsk. You're in too precarious of a situation to be getting pompous with me." She shook her finger at him as if he was a scolded child.

"Can we discuss this rationally, Aster?"

She started laughing hysterically and it crawled down my throat like a spider on a tight web.

"I'm a ghostly witch and you think this can be rational?" She cackled like her namesake and floated above the floor a few inches as I speared him with a look which would hopefully have him not make any further remarks like that.

"See, Kenrick, this is why I treasure you so. You continue to amaze me and I'll never be bored with you."

He wouldn't be stopped. "Why can't you just be dead like anyone else?"

"Shut up, Kenrick!" I snapped.

"Renata understands that you don't say these things to a scorned woman who has enough power to turn you into a monster, you should heed the warnings."

"Aster, go into the light or whatever else spirits do when they've exhausted themselves on the earth with mortals who have forgotten you."

"Kenrick!" I yelled as she turned toward him with the sheers suddenly in her hands.

He didn't even flinch. Please let me be dreaming again.

"I see what you are doing, my love," she said as she began wiping her sheers clean, using the apron tied around her small waist.

"If you don't see that I don't want you then you are blind."

A tickle of laughter came from the ghost again but this time she carried the mirth of a toddler with her. I never wanted to hear her laugh again.

"You don't want your lover to know what all of this is about. Would you rather I killed you so she'd never know your little secret, *cher*?"

His face went blank and I could see she had made a point. I was finally going to be told what was going on and why Aster said Kenrick was over a hundred years old.

"Tell her," the ghost goaded softly. "Let us move on to better things."

He pressed his lips together so tightly that I waited for the blood to stream out of them.

"Tell her, you asinine man," Aster shrieked.

"If I'm such an ass then why do you want me so badly?" he dared to ask.

"You want to die, don't you?" Her eyes almost popped out with her anger at him.

"If it will end this farce of a life, then yes, please do so. Then you can go straight to hell where you belong in the bed of the devil himself."

Lightning struck outside but I could have sworn it came from her and not the bawling sky. Silence fell until the thunder boomed across our tense figures while we waited for her next move.

"Tell her or I will and my version will not be laced with the sweetness of your tongue," she whispered so softly I felt the edge of ice in it.

Something had to have passed across her features because he shrank into himself right in front of us. I couldn't see her face but knew she was staring him down and I felt content with it. If it made him have that reaction then I wouldn't want to draw her attention back to myself. Instead, I needed to look around and figure a way out of this.

His voice was timid as he began to talk. "Aster probably told you that I was her love from a century ago but the truth is she tried to seduce me but I wouldn't have her tainted body in my bed."

Aster spun as if on a spinning top and Kenrick was flung backward with the force of her blow. How had she done all this as a spirit? She wasn't mortal so she shouldn't have been able to do that to him. Were the stories of spirits channeling energy true? Did she have the ability to collect enough to keep moving until she exhausted her metaphysical storage? If it was true, then we could take away enough power to make her unable to complete the spell or harm us much further. The whirlwind she had created earlier should have drained her to a point where it would have delayed her actions. Staring at her hovering figure, her motions were a bit stilted, as if it was a bad copy of a movie playing.

Kenrick just lay there, looking up at her as if he was daring her to do anything else. That man either had the biggest balls I had ever seen or he was the deadest one.

"Do you want me to stay down here as you complete the story, my dear," he bit out in disgust.

I saw him spit blood right past her seething form. I was glad it hadn't hit her for fear that it would have given her more power. Maybe he just meant it as the insult it represented and nothing more.

"It would be lovely to have you at my feet but it's not dignified," she said sweetly.

"Dignified? You're a whore of Satan and now you're too much of a high class lay to let me grovel at your invisible feet. That is rich."

"Silence, you cowering mongrel! I have had enough of your voice. I will tell her the story and you will sit and watch the horror of it cross her pretty face as she sees what you really are."

"Can I help him up while you tell the story?" I asked her.

"Why does it matter to you?" she asked out of surprise.

"It bothers me to see him in such a condition. Besides, if I'm to see the true Kenrick Giles then shouldn't I be able to look him in the eyes when you reveal him to me?"

"Quite right, Renata. Go ahead and help him up, but no untying him. That part amuses me." She waved me forward and I skirted her as best as I could while shuffling around the furniture to get him.

He looked so angry and defensive when I got to where he lay vulnerable and bleeding. His strong arms had been tied at the wrists and then tied to the rope that secured his ankles to the bottom rung of the wooden chair. He was trussed up like a pig going to market. The thought of him being unable to stop her was what Aster wanted from this staged scene.

I would have to tip the chair back up without it sliding out from under me. My arm strength wasn't up to doing this gracefully. Standing over his head, I slowly pushed it into a more upright position and whispered in his ear, "Any ideas?"

"Nothing other than getting us out of here. You?"

Aster looked over at us as I kept up with my turtle-like progress. "What are you two whispering about?"

Kenrick grunted and said, "She's making unladylike noises, and I'm laughing at her."

"Do you think that she is not strong enough to help out such a virile man?" Aster questioned.

"Yes, if given the proper motivation plus the adrenaline to back it up. At this moment, she is too frightened to properly save herself let alone anyone else."

I finished my task and reached around to place a palm in between his open legs as I pushed him firmly back into place.

"Watch it, buddy. I'm not the one tied up for the big event," I said softly in his ear.

His gaze flickered down to my unbound breasts bouncing against my nightshirt and he winked at me. I wanted to drop him back on the floor.

"Renata, you and I have some work to do with this one. He seems to have lost his tongue and his manners since I left him last."

"Why do you want him if he's so much of a cur?" I asked, using her own words back on her.

"The man can kiss like the devil himself and I won't deny my heart still leaps at the sight of those liquid eyes."

I blushed at the mention of the kiss, even if the context was ghoulish.

"So, you have tasted the dear lady, have you, Kenrick?"

He said nothing and just glared daggers at her.

"Maybe you can hold your tongue, at least in this moment, but you had no problems using it on our new friend. I'm jealous but pleased at this confirmation."

"Jealousy should be beneath a dead woman," Kenrick said with a mocking grin.

Aster's eyes flashed, and she made a gesture with her nimble fingers. Blood beaded from the corner of his lips where the smirk had been just a second ago. He spat it away from her, and she laughed as if he'd just offered her a posy or graced her with a compliment.

"Check his restraints," Aster said as she turned back to her book of secrets.

Placing my hand on top of the knot at the chair bottom, I saw something flicker from the corner of my eyes. It appeared to be a small piece of glass he was using to cut into the rope that held him in place. Looking down at his feet, I saw a more jagged piece and palmed it as I feigned looking over each inch of the rope. As my hands slid upward, and in a more sexual area, I slithered my shard into his empty hand and met his rapidly moving eyes as they tried to keep up with all movements in the room. He gave a slight nod before Aster gave us a roving glance as she read another page of lines and directions.

"This one won't let you go either, my dear. You either slighted her or she's more witch than I first guessed."

"I'm no witch, Aster," I retorted.

"Maybe not, but you possess enough of a gift to make things easier for my transformation."

Once I was done, she motioned me back over to my original spot as she waited for my full attention. Gazing to the attic door, I saw a dresser had been moved just over the doorframe as to make opening it more of a challenge. I was strong enough to shove it aside but could she be strong enough to stop me from fleeing? That was the question and I hoped why he kept barbing her with his silver tongue. Once I was seated, I saw a few smears of blood from my stumbling effort with Kenrick. She saw where I looked and shook her head at me.

"Don't waste too much, as I'll need some of it before morning."

"Enough of this cryptic talk, just tell me what the hell is going on," I said a bit too brisk for someone in this precarious situation.

"Yes, the night is getting old, and this must be completed before the sun touches the ground with its full rays."

It gave us an estimate of how long we had to distract her or to stop this madness entirely.

"It all began when I was a young woman who fell for the handsome farmer who helped tend the household lands."

"In a land far, far away," interrupted Kenrick.

That got him another metaphysical slap across the face. This one didn't throw him down but it left the impression of a small hand across his right cheek. Could she be weakening or just concentrating harder on her target?

Once she turned her back on him, I noticed his

hands moving against the restraints. He nodded at me and I understood he wanted me to keep her attention as he attempted to use both shards to break his bonds.

"Go on with your history lesson, Aster." I waved a hand in the air.

"Back then flirting was not as bold but I did what I could to attract him to me. I saw him gaze on the bodies of the ladies who came to the house and knew from tales that he wasn't as virginal as my father had hoped. One night, I watched him with a lady from a few houses down and knew I had to be the next one for his attention."

It was hard to keep eye contact with someone who could be seen through but I managed to keep her facing me. It was sinister how she had stalked her prey for this long and wouldn't let her death be the end of the hunt.

"I began to experiment with spells and potions but my gift was lacking where most spells were concerned. The only one I was effective at casting happened to be the one which brought me back as a ghost after I had mistakenly taken my own life in the process. Playing with magic is not all games as some of the best results can have the highest price."

"Tell me how because I am intrigued to be speaking to a ghost," I asked.

"Intrigued? This makes me like my choice in people to possess even better, but we'll get to that. Kenrick wasn't picking anyone to court so I pursued him to distraction. Earning enough money to purchase the more exotic plants, I began making the love potion I came across. I wasn't going to use the first few batches on my own love as it might not be safe, so I sold it to the foolish girls in the neighborhood who wanted to have the more rich gentlemen become enraptured with them. They wanted my potions to obtain wealth and standing in the material world where I wanted love, passion, and the freedom to practice.

My father shunned anything not conventionally Christian so I hid most of my dealings. Sometimes I believe he purely wished not to see what I was becoming. I didn't need his approval but I needed him to support my life as I sought out one of my own making. He even refused to believe how I had come to die that unfortunate night. Since I had become a spirit, I saw my own funeral plus the life on the estate those many years afterward. I went into a state of solitude for many of those years as things were not worth the effort to make myself known. Then you brought me back to full consciousness."

She was gazing directly at me and it spread a shudder across my skin. "How did I accomplish that?"

"Your power breathed into this house and shook me awake from my years of boredom. Out of all of the people in this area, I had found the one person who could get me out of these self-induced doldrums and back to living. You were meant to save me. I honestly believe it. And when you didn't run screaming from the house at the first hint of ghostly energy, you silently confirmed my belief that I could get on with what I was meant to be."

"What is so fabulous about me? I have life crippling visions that make every moment a danger as I never know when I'll succumb and blackout. I'm a mess and no one wants to be involved in such an insane way to live. Friends walked away and would-be lovers ran as fast as their feet could carry them as they realized what a nightmare I was. No one in their right mind would want my life."

Kenrick interrupted again. "Aster is far out of her right mind and always has been. She has admitted to being a practicing witch and that is enough proof for me."

"Kenrick, you would be wise to be quiet. Don't make me strike you again."

I met his eyes and he nodded at me again before twisting his hands in a manner to where I could see the remaining strand of rope left between his legs. A jolt of excitement ripped from my heart as I got a glimmer of hope, but I schooled my face not to show it as I had to keep the ghost talking.

"Having seen the positive effect of the potion on other men, I brewed up one last batch to use on my intended. That day, I made the mixture in the graveyard, as no one would be likely to find me there and I had already fashioned a story of being busy for the next few hours so my father wouldn't be concerned with me. It was perfect until I met up with Kenrick the same night. Things hadn't gone as planned."

Remembering that part of my visions and her watching him from the tree line, she finalized the plan for her last move. The next one had been her clipping off the ingredients she needed. It was all falling into place. All this meant that it had to be true about how old Kenrick was but not what had kept him alive this long.

"I see realization dawning in your eyes, Renata. You see where this leads, do you not?"

"The visions you showed me were of the day this all occurred," I stated simply.

"Yes, but the first vision was not of my doing. When I saw what you could do, some of it was accidentally transferred to you as you were more emotional. I apologize but it gave me the idea to show you that I really hadn't meant you any harm, either of you."

"This tells me what your intentions were but something happened, didn't it? Something got messed up so badly, it not only backfired but killed you."

"Correct."

"The bitchy witch didn't think that I had what it took to tell her no. Did you, Aster?"

With a flash, she flung her arm out, causing the chair to fling back a good two feet before he was slammed to the ground. I went to check him out but she got in front of me and held up a single finger.

"Do not force my hand," she stated calmly.

Power crept from her in invisible figures and poked at my quivering skin. I couldn't help him if I got knocked out, so I had to remain as calm as possible. I learned that in a self-defense course the school had sponsored one night. But they never covered how to protect yourself from a spirit who was after you.

"Continue your story."

"Yes, time is fading. I'll finish my directions as I tell the end of the tale."

Floating back to the book, she bent down to collect all of her items in a precise order on the platter. Not noticing that Kenrick had begun to move slowly.

"Meeting Kenrick in the greenhouse had been a way to have us out of sight and was a place of power for me. I had brought wine from the cellar and had the potion hidden in the pocket of my apron. Toasting my successful crop, I shared a glass with my love. I was about to pour the potion into his glass when an unexpected storm began to brew. The thunder had scared me, causing me to drop the bottle, as I began to undo my dress. Kenrick being a gentleman went to retrieve it for me. Sadly, he recognized the bottle from one I had sold a girl earlier in the week. I hadn't known he had been watching, so I was surprised at him throwing it across the room."

Seemingly satisfied with the contents she had arranged, she began to light the two candles that had remained untouched, until now. Her eyes were closed and she said something under her breath as fire caught to both wicks.

"He knew what I had planned and would have no part in it. I was stricken with unrequited love for this man who dared to call me all sorts of foul names. I was a witch but not a murdering harlot after his soul. When I tried to tell him my true intentions, how much I loved him, he tossed me to the floor of the greenhouse like trash.

"He departed as I cried, leaving me in the storm to fend for myself. He was no gentleman, my love. But I still wanted him, badly. Knowing I could fix things, I grabbed up what was left in my bottle and ran to the cemetery to see if more had been left in my hidden cauldron. I was heartbroken but I saw he had gone up into his room and could see him getting ready for bed. The cad was going to pay for abandoning me. I cast out the words in Latin that would cause my demise. If this man could go to bed after leaving me to weep, then the only satisfaction he would ever get was from those dreams. I vowed he would never find love in the waking moments of his remaining days. He would never feel the depth of true love if it did not come from me. This man would pay for scorning my gifts and my heart."

Aster's form blinked in and out so rapidly it was a strobe of lights before my unbelieving eyes. She was reliving the amount of hurt and rage that had changed her life and taken her into the spirit world.

"As I completed the spell, I was struck by lightning, thus ending my short life and giving him the essence of immortality. But something in that spell also turned me into a metaphysical being who watched as the world evolved around me. Sticking to his side, I saw the spell had indeed made him pay for his sins against me. He was turned from a living breathing man into a sort of incubus who only lived when feeding off the sexual energy of a woman. You can imagine my surprise that I could invade his dreams to get the satisfaction I craved as a living woman but he devoured any strength I had at the moment of entry. I could only visit him once the energy was enough to join him again, but then something strange happened to stop my visits to his bedchamber. It was you. That was when I knew for certain I could use you to come back. You would save me from the useless world I had been cursed to and take me back to the land of the living. If I could get enough energy, and the right spell, I could bring myself back to life in your body and still use the potion on Kenrick. I want to thank you, Renata, as you are about to make the ultimate sacrifice for me."

Chapter Fourteen

She intended to kill me so she could have my body. Aster would use me to take over the house, the money, and force Kenrick into falling madly in love with her. She was insane and about to snuff me out as a way to make her fantasy life come to fruition.

Then she was on me in a heartbeat as she drew her sheers up. Flinging my hands up in a defensive move, she embedded the point into the palm of one hand in her attempt to stab me in the chest with the wicked blades. Then I heard a roar that had nothing to do with the circulating storm outside and everything to do with the man who was advancing on the altar Aster had made for her ceremony.

I thought he was going to yank me away from her but her form wasn't thick enough for us to shove her away. I could feel the pressure of the blade burning into my right palm but that's where her energy was being focused. Kicking and shoving had no effect on her as her eyes bulged from their shadowy sockets at her level of concentration. Hearing a crash, Kenrick grabbed at the platter and kicked the furniture over as he bellowed at her to release me. She didn't. In fact, the grip on my neck increased as I fought the pressure at my hand. She wanted me to be out cold so I couldn't fight her anymore. Did it mean she was running out of energy from this onslaught? God, I hoped so.

Yelling for her, he dumped the contents of the plate and broke it over his knee. Aster screamed so loudly my ears felt as if they would burst. The crushing embrace at my throat decreased as she took in the damage he inflicted on her things. He stomped on the platter and the more action he took, the weaker she became by the destruction of her power items. Shards of ceramic mixed with green globs while he pummeled the contents into the bare wood of the floor under us. Spots danced before my eyes as my lungs scrambled for oxygen. Another ear-splitting scream emitted from her throat and she faded away, leaving me to slump on the floor, gasping for air.

Coming to me, he kneeled. "We have to get out of here before she materializes again."

"What are we going to do? She could appear at any time and kill us both."

Shaking his head, he said, "She could have done that a million times over the last hundred years but she didn't. She can't let me go so I'll be kept alive while she tries for another way to cast the damned spell on me."

"Do you have an idea on how to stop her? For good?"

"She mentioned the graveyard and the cemetery as being places of power, so we can try there."

"No way in hell am I going to put myself in her place of power so she can try to kill me again. Are you crazy?"

"We have to, don't you see? One of those places is where she placed her essence so she could come back. If we find out where it's hidden, then we can destroy it and her with it."

"It's insane."

"Have any better ideas?" he inquired wryly.

I had to admit that I didn't.

"Keep pressure on your hand, and we'll grab a towel on the way out of here."

He pulled me to my feet and led me out of the attic and to his room. There he tied a washrag around my blood covered hand and slid his slippers over to me. Sliding them on felt wrong as I had dried blood on my skin but it was the least of our concerns right now.

Running outside, he held my good hand while we trekked into the storm to see if she had anything hidden in the greenhouse. It was deathly quiet as we entered the room and he started up the flame on the propane lantern stationed in the humid room. The natural glow did nothing to assuage my fears as I looked for signs of the ghost around us. He was investigating every nook and cranny so I closed my eyes and went back over the images she had shared with me previously. I saw the platter being hidden, where the book had been kept, and the old shelf she had used now housed garden tools.

"Here." I pointed it out. "This is where she had her plants and that shelf is where she hid her things."

Sweeping the items aside, he looked for signs of anything she could have left. Her original diary wasn't there and only the more recent items had been left behind after so many years of use.

"Had it been cleaned out?"

"If she has the power to become material then she has to have something around here to build from. Let's go to the graveyard and see if she has something hidden there."

Nodding, I saw him grab up a small citronella

candle from the shelf and the old lighter stationed behind it. I let him lead the way into the darkness to the small outcropping of stones that lined the sacred area.

"Be careful," he said as we picked our way around the stones to get to where the marble had Aster's named scratched off of it.

He used the extended covering of one of the cracked stones as a dry place for the candle and lit it in between curses at the rain pattering around us. Saying a word of thanks to whoever left a lighter instead of a box of wooden matches, I felt a bit better when the flame stayed in motion as he looked around the witch's marker. He reached just under the weeping willow tree when I heard a snap. Screaming above the unnatural wind, I saw a flash just as a broken branch smashed into Kenrick's bent over form, knocking him into the soggy ground.

Using what little there remained of my night vision, I saw blood streaming down a gash on the side of his handsome face. How many more blows to the head could this man sustain? He was breathing but no muscles flinched under my touch at his injury. Knowing Aster had been the cause for the tree to lay him out, she had to be hidden around here.

"What are you waiting for, Aster?" I bellowed into the wind that wrapped around us like a current of icy fingers. She was gathering enough energy to reform in front of us.

The wind became her laughter as she made herself more substantial. "Are you in a hurry to leave this world, Renata?"

I stood in the rain, covered in dirt and grass, bleeding, aching, and at the end of my rope as I held onto any semblance of hope for getting us out of this as ourselves. No matter what she had done to Kenrick, or what she had in store for him, the waiting was unbearable.

"I'm sick of the games, so do what you have to do and get it over with." I pulled Kenrick onto my lap.

"My poor man has gone and gotten himself injured again. Now he won't be able to see the light change in your eyes as I take over your life force. Maybe he likes you too much to see that happen anyway."

"He doesn't love me, so you're wasting your breath," I replied to the shadow thickening in front of me.

"I believe you are wrong on this account. In all the years where I have watched, he has never come to you like he did to the other women. He visited you several times and would tease you about your lack of understanding of what he was doing to you. You had to have realized that your visions were increasing as he fed from your slumbering form. He had your body and your release as he made you believe you were safe in your chaste bed. What lies."

"I have seen no proof your words are any more true than his were. You state you have gone about changing people's lives to your own satisfaction, so how are you any different than what you claim he is?"

"Can you argue with me over you being visited by him on more than one occasion while you lay down to slumber?"

There was no way to keep from heating at the thoughts of what he had done to me in those dreams.

"I can feel your arousal," she stated and then laughed. "Do not be embarrassed as I too wish to feel his touch on my skin."

"But you have to get that skin first."

"Exactly," she said with more happiness than I wished her to have after my factual words.

"Am I going to be myself anymore or will you take over everything, killing me?"

"You will remain as a piece of your soul will stay attached to this body, but you will have no control in things I decide to do. You will simply be part of my consciousness and nothing more. Eventually, that part of you may die off as your will gives way under my strength but it won't be for many years."

"So, I'll be less than you are right now?"

"Yes, but at least you'll still have the items you have come to love. The estate will be cared for, the money will be there to take care of our needs, and you'll be in the arms of the man you have fallen in love with. What more could you ask for in this situation?"

"You seem very sure of our feelings for each other. We aren't victims of your potions, so you shouldn't be this secure in your plan."

"But, you will be, or at least, Kenrick will be. We already have our feelings so all I need is for him to love me as I continue on in your body."

Before I could scream at her for the idiotic game she was playing, she threw a blast of glowing orange power directly at my chest. I barely had time to breath before pain so intense took me to a place in my mind where only the cries of hell echoed. The feeling turned into a ripping sensation as if I was being yanked from my seam in the blanket of life. Crying out in my mind, the sound never made it out of my silent lips. Did the jerking move me over so she'd have more room inside of my body or could she be tearing my soul out of its place in the universe? This agony was worse than all of the visions combined into one ball of lava that encased me in a heat so hot it felt as if I was sizzling in the blast of one hundred suns.

No longer feeling the sway of the wind around me, the stab of pain at my cut feet, or the pressure of the man in my lap, there was only white noise as I was surrounded by gray thick enough to lie in. No sunny mental room for me in this cursed prison. This woman had no sunshine to share. She slipped into me like a brand new wool coat, warm and ready to be broken in. It felt awful. Trying to cry out was useless as no sound emanated from my lungs. I was no longer myself. She had taken everything away from me in a single blast of ever after. My drab gray walls shifted as she settled herself into my body. Then all I heard was her laughter.

"My dear, I feel your distress. I will be kind and let you see the world through my new eyes so you know what is taking place. Just open your metaphysical shield at any time and you will be a part of my actions. I cannot allow anything else for you as I can't give you room to be naughty."

Flickering the part of me that recognized her power, I opened up. It was like looking directly at searing coals with the first glance. Blinking, I concentrated on what was before her. She was playing with Kenrick's hair as it moved in the wind which clung to them. He looked so peaceful, for a man she had knocked out. It was as if he was sleeping. Sighing in her head, she let go of him and waved symbols in front of herself in the air. I could just see the burning edge of runes in the atmosphere as she cast a new spell.

Everything around us blurred. I kept blinking but it was all distorted, like oil smeared glasses.

When I could focus again, we were on my bedroom floor, back in the house. The bitch could teleport us as if she were still a shimmering ghost and not a spiritual possessor of a human body. Things were still in the disarray from earlier and worse than what I had recalled from my peek out of the covers. Letting Kenrick's head slip to the rug under us, she left him there as she went about righting the room. Time had a different meaning in my dislocated soul. It could blur with speed or creep like a snail, depending on how hard I concentrated on following the actions of my betraying body.

Her strength was also more than I had anticipated. Why couldn't she have had a normal person's characteristics? This defied too many natural laws. Would it stay this way or would it wane with her actions, like her spirit form did? She was even able to circulate a small enough amount of wind in the room to sweep the glass aside as she noticed her borrowed feet were bleeding again. Taking a tissue from the table beside the bed, she leaned down and wiped away the blood congealed to the side of his beautiful face. She wasn't able to remove it all so she had to get a wet cloth from the bathroom to remove the evidence of the attack.

Once she became satisfied with the results, she struggled when she realized her new body was a bit weaker than her power form. Annoyed, she struggled over how to get an unwilling man back onto the bed a few feet above the ground where he lay. After several attempts, she shoved the mattress back to the floor and dragged him up onto it by inching him as she pulled under his shoulders. I felt better when she let him slump against her in her last pull of new muscles on his sleeping form. It gave me hope that she had not taken this into consideration when choosing her host. My visions would not keep her safe in this shell and I wondered how she would react to one once she wore herself out to the point of mental exhaustion, if she was able to retain that part of me when she was forced to keep my soul in residence. Having bones and muscles to now deal with, she seemed more awkward in her movements when her magic wasn't supporting her totally, especially for someone who had been able to hover with only the strength of her vengeful spirit.

Her weariness caused her new eyes to flutter as she fought the fatigue of a mortal body. Only being able to see life as it happened before her eyes, I was even more limited as to what I could do when she took that away from me. Would I sleep while she slept or would I just be held in a purgatory of the witch's making? I would soon find out. She curled up against his lean form, pulling comfort and satisfaction from him simply being there after all these years. Lashes fluttered as the view of him beside the witch possessed form of my body was taken away and the gray slithered back in abundance.

****

"Renata, do you hear me?" Came a whispered voice in the fog of my prison.

Feeling as if I was back in a dream, I went to roll back over and ignore the person who dared to wake me when I felt so freaking tired. When I didn't feel the sheets against my cool body, I looked around to see nothing but the drab of gray that seemed to choke at me. It all hit me in that moment and I could feel my panic growing as the fog seemed to get closer to me. But it couldn't. I had to remind myself that I wasn't being crowded because I had no real body to push upon. I did but she had taken it away from me like a body snatcher from a creepy old movie.

Then the voice interrupted my chaotic thoughts again.

"Renata, are you still in there? Please be in there somewhere?"

Mentally, I answered, "I'm here."

"Damn, I was afraid she had completely killed you off."

"I'm not much better," I informed him.

"Your spirit still holds a spark and that's good enough for now."

"How are you hearing me or even able to get past her to talk to me when she's taken my free will away from me?"

"She didn't take something into consideration," he hinted.

"What would that be?"

"She's asleep and I'm still cursed."

"Look, I'm tired of playing words games with people. Just spit it out," I retorted.

"If the only power I have is when your body is asleep, then we still have a chance to get you back to where you should be and her in literal hell."

"Kenrick, how are you going to dream up an escape route? She cast a spell to take over my body and I'm stuck in this corner until she chooses to release me. Us having sex is not going to get me any closer to the escape hatch."

"Think about it. She stopped us the last time but

she knows you're skimming around in her subconscious. She knows I have the power to enter a woman's mind once she's asleep, so why can't I try to play a little game and see what comes about? What will it hurt? I'm laid out and couldn't reach you until she was into a deeper realm of relaxation and now is my chance. I'm not sure how long I'll be out, so we may not have this chance tomorrow night. If it works, but we have to regroup, then we'll try again in a couple of days when her guard is back down. Now that she's taken human form, she can't avoid sleep as your body won't last very long under extreme fatigue."

"What I'd like to know is if she still has my ability to have random visions? If we can get her stressed out enough, then she may have one that throws her for a loop. It took me ages to be able to gain control of this power and she has no idea what it entails. At least, that's how she talks about it," I voiced my concern.

"I say we try and see what effects it has on the big bad witch."

"Fine, but how can you dream about me when I don't have a body for you to take advantage of anymore?" I was trying not to sound offended at the fact he was admitting to what he had been doing but in a way where we could discuss it rationally. "By the way, if we get out of this, you and I are going to have a long talk about what you did to me."

"Do you hate me for what I am?" he asked with a slice of pain in the words.

I waited a moment longer than I should have to answer, but I had to be honest. "No, but it doesn't mean I'm okay with it either."

"Renata, this is the wrong way to tell you but I

want you back in your body, as you should be, so I can properly court you."

That took me by surprise.

"Renata, are you still there, honey?"

"I'm here."

"Please, say something," he said so softly I barely registered what he'd requested.

"Get us out of this nightmare and I'll give you a few days to explain everything to me, in detail. Agreed?"

"Agreed! And I'm not the monster under your bed. I'm the lover coming to give you a wet dream."

Chapter Fifteen

I focused my thinking on him but when nothing happened, I centered on myself instead. I had to have a body for him to come to me, so that made more sense. Feeling a warm spot where I would imagine my middle to be, I pushed it outward. The elastic feeling was uncomfortable but bearable as I saw my legs begin to form under me. Wiggling a solid looking toe, I heard a laugh too masculine to be mine.

"I knew you could figure it out," Kenrick's voice said to me.

"Some things, like information, are better when shared," I stated truthfully.

"Sex is one of those things," he retorted with humor riding his words.

Shaking my head, that wasn't present yet, I was not going to waste energy arguing with him. Taking the feeling centered at my spine, I mentally pushed it so the tingle of it rode over what I hoped would be my hair covered scalp. Messy tresses came into view and a thrill came over me as I had successfully made myself materialize. Aster wasn't the only one powerful enough, or stubborn enough, to make magic happen. As if on cue, Kenrick began to walk to me from the gray distance and he was clothed exactly like when we'd started our date. This sleek casual look was sexy and I had no problem with him taking it back on in my mind.

If this occurred in his mind and not my twisted one. As he got closer, I saw he was indeed barefoot, so I asked him who happened to be in charge here.

"Well, we're doing this as your body sleeps, so I would say you have the control over this. Why do you ask?"

"I wondered if I was picking out our clothes," I shyly answered.

"Who said you were wearing clothes, sweetheart?"

Looking down, I saw I had indeed come into full view and I stood stark naked under his heated gaze.

"Shit!"

"Don't get upset. I've seen it all before, remember?"

My hands went to cover what they were able to and I fought the insecure feelings of boldly standing here with nothing to really cover myself.

"This is not how I wanted to show up," I confirmed out loud.

"It's fine, really. And it answers part of our questions as you didn't even think of making clothes appear and you still don't have any on. That must be my fault."

"Do you mind handling that?" I asked with a bit of annoyance in my voice.

"Yes, I can certainly handle that." And he was on me in a stolen heartbeat.

He began kissing me as if he'd been starving for years. Taking possession of my mouth, he tasted every centimeter of it before deepening the kiss to swooning level. It buried every kiss he'd given me so far and I was clutching at the front of his shirt as he made me shudder under the aggressive action of his wicked tongue. Was he drinking my sexual essence in through my open mouth?

As we were in a dream, and I was stuck in mental limbo, there was no furniture or walls to lean against. Just when my legs wobbled, he scooped me up before laying me on the cloudlike floor of my prison. His hands went everywhere as soon as I got out of his protective hold. He started touching every part of me and all at the same time. He found erogenous zones I hadn't known existed. Even the inside of my elbow laid bare to our desires.

Sweeping his clothes back off, I was in awe of his lean farmer's body and toned muscular build. He was gorgeous. Running my hands over him, I drew nonexistent patterns across the skin that I couldn't tell was warm or cold. He was just there, above me, as his gaze burned down my flesh. One of his hands played at my sensitive nipples as the other slid down my legs and into the softer crevice of my thighs. As he nudged my legs apart, I gasped when he nipped my breast. His teeth and tongue played with one as his hand tugged almost painfully at the other. If that was too much, he leaned himself beside me where his other hand could slide over my lower half as his weight was taken off of it. No one had ever paid this much attention to my body, not even a physician.

His mouth captured the gasp emitted from my parted lips when his slender fingers played at my core. Digging my hands into his shoulders, I held on as he had me crying out for the release that would roll over me at any moment. After a few deft strokes inside of me, my back arched with the amount of pressure which caught me in a sexual whirlwind. With his hand still playing, his teeth bit into a nipple almost too painfully but it drove the orgasm to tighten around his fingers, capturing him. But still, he did not stop. Just when I thought I would lose the body I had made from my lack of focus, his lower half moved and he thrust into me. I was impaled by his manhood and gave myself over to his movements. My mind exploded as another orgasm claimed me. Then a scream erupted so loud that my concentration was completely blown away.

My eyes were now open, seeing the bedroom, as Aster awoke from our erotic dream. I had been so close to feeling his release that it was excruciating to have it all vanish under her seething anger. I prayed he had taken enough energy from my body to help us get out of this and keep us alive. I'd be happy if I could at least get back into my body, even if it meant I was to be haunted for my rebellion.

"How dare you!" she screeched at us.

He vanished, and I appeared back in my drab box with no body of my own. Wanting to cry, I could only feel myself shrinking away.

If I could see what was going on outside of my cell, then I'd know if Kenrick had come to and if he was safe from her wrath. Then an idea came to me. If I had been able to fabricate myself a dream body then maybe I could force her to share her eyesight or hearing. Centering myself, picturing where my chakras were, I made my will into a glowing ball of color and shoved it upward. After a second, I heard a gasp and it was my own voice. Grasping that triumph like a ray of hope, I pulled it to me. And then I could see Kenrick still lying prone on the bed. His soft breath came to the ears opening to me. He seemed okay and she hadn't taken it out on him, yet. Was she aware of what I had done or maybe too busy using her unearthly strength to maintain her will over mine? I heard her whispering to him.

"My sweet betraying love, what were you up to? Were you using her to gain enough power to come back to me, or to conquer my power?"

Nothing came from him, not even a motion of him waking.

Her eyes were heavy again, as she hadn't had enough time to recuperate, especially with us using some of her power to bring Kenrick to full health. A fleeting thought poked at me and I didn't want to give it a second appraisal, but it was valid. What if he had seduced me to get himself out of this and not to save us both? Would he do that to me after what had happened? After he had admitted to having feelings for me? Time would tell if I was truly someone of importance to him and God save me if I was wrong. While Aster fell back asleep, I waited and conserved my energy.

****

Time passed in bits and pieces as I hung in the grip of her possession of me. I'd seen her get up and take care of a few human things that shocked her to deal with. Kenrick remained comatose, but his lungs moved to keep him going. The steady pulse at his extended neck had reassured me he was only healing himself as we regrouped. I fought my own hysteria as Aster only allowed me subtle glimpses of her as she walked the estate. I wasn't going to waste what I had on little peaks when I had a feeling things were only going to get worse.

She didn't go to the greenhouse or the graveyard,

skirting them to see everything else. That felt odd to me. If either was a place of power then I would have thought she would go there to step up her potion. Instead, she brought the items she had grabbed from around the yard and had taken the armload of it back to the kitchen.

Maybe she had gone to the greenhouse and had blocked my sight because there were things on the counter that were not to be found in the pantry. Not knowing enough about plants to recognize them, I focused on the piece of paper showing from her book. Yes, it was her love potion. In small handwritten print at the bottom, it said the dose was strongest if taken within twenty-four hours of it hitting full potency. It was a good detail to know. She either planned to slide it down his throat while he remained asleep or she was confident enough that he would be awake in the next thirty-six hours. Him being asleep gave me less of a chance to save him unless he was stronger when joined with a woman's sleep induced mind.

If he was awake and in good health, then he could struggle until he could get free. Maybe she didn't have the human strength to stop him from leaving. That was it! She planned to get it down him before he had his full senses about him. At that point, she'd have his utter devotion. There would be no stopping the rest of her plans as she took over the property as me. Then I wondered if she had taken Mr. White into consideration. Would he show up, and would she have to pretend to be me? She'd have to be convincing but then again, he didn't know me well enough to press the point. This was so infuriating. I had no more power here than I did in the middle of a heart-stopping vision.

The doorbell chimed and Aster was shocked into motion. When she opened the door, a courier stood there with a large manila envelope. She signed for the paperwork and I snuck a peek at the address of the law firm Mr. White owned. Attached to the outside of the large envelope was a smaller white one. Ripping it open, she continued to allow me to share whatever was about to happen.

Ms. Barkely,

I have been unable to visit in person due to damage from the recent storm but wanted you to have a final look at the paperwork included in the will. It only has a few differences from the first set as it is more up to date with the finances. Please look over this and I will be there to see you tomorrow night for your final decision.

Sincerely,

Mr. White

Aster spun around in glee as she registered how much money she would be cashing in on. She stopped in her merriment long enough to dance around the house as she looked for the first set of papers left with me. Sadly, she found them and her joy was palpable at the amount of money she would be entitled to once she had everything finalized. What a bitch! After checking on the unchanged state of her handsome victim, she went back to the kitchen to assume duties on the potion she was excited to brew. But I'd been disappointed to see her weave some kind of spell over the door before she had come downstairs. She'd know if he got up while she stayed occupied elsewhere.

She allowed me to see her detailed work in mixing all of the ingredients, even the emphasis she put into grinding some of the plants into an unrecognizable paste at the bottom of her mortar. The mixture began to brew over the low heat of the gas stove in one of the copper pots that usually hung on the rack above the bar side of the countertops.

The mixture resembled creamed spinach and was left to warm as she went into the library to get the two champagne flutes that had been placed on an antique silver tray by the large bookcase. She ran a delicate finger around the rim to make it sing as her building joy resonated through the staircase after looking in on Kenrick. However, her feelings of paranoia were simmering under the surface and that was a good sign. If she'd just left him unsupervised, it might show her cockiness but it would also show him as being more injured than I had originally guessed.

She poured some of the wine from my interrupted undate into one of the flutes and took a long sip as if she just realized how much she had missed it since her body had died. I'm sure she had indulged in alcohol when she was young, as she'd been responsible for the neighbor's crop flourishing under her care. Her age would have no bearing on it, like it did now with the more modern laws of my day. Besides, it was naive to believe Aster could be anything other than an opportunist when it came to any material item she set her sights on.

Once the brew had come to the proper temperature, she let it cool as she drank down more of the wine. Since it would take a few moments, she used the time to tidy up the items around the kitchen, even humming that insane tune from before while salting the green stain from the surface of the warm-toned bowl. When done, she scooped some of the slimy mixture into the bottom of the unused flute before pouring the remaining wine equally between her glass and the goop laden one. It looked disgusting. I couldn't imagine how she believed she could get the stuff down the throat of a man that wasn't conscious enough to swallow on his own accord.

Swirling the mixture around with a silver spoon, she walked both glasses upstairs and back into my bedroom. Kenrick laid in a tousled heap on the bed, but it seemed he had moved around a little bit. One of his feet peeked out from the corner of the covers, and his face now looked toward the high ceiling. Stopping for a moment, she paused at the spelled threshold, taking in his masculine form as she told herself he would soon belong to her and her alone. What she felt for this man went beyond simple love at first sight. She had been stalking him for years as her largest prey. Would the success of the evening end the passion which had kept her going for so long? When he woke loving her, would it be enough? Her wants, drive, and insecurity were so profound that I felt shredded by the chaotic way she had fought to have him. She truly had let vengeance drive her insane.

Being who she was, no formal ceremony would be called for to set this trap. She was just going to curl up beside him and get down enough of the vile potion to have him wake as her passionate lover. She arranged herself in a settled pile in the same spot I had been when I had been captured by her. How interesting? Kenrick's head was held up so she could take my pillow and place it gently under his lower neck in a way that opened up his throat. It would make this go easier, if she didn't end up getting it down his windpipe and into his lungs.

Once she had him in a better placement, she closed her eyes tightly and it looked as if she was saying a prayer. Straining my power, I could make out the words of a poem, from many years ago.

> *You'll love me yet!—and I can tarry*
> *Your love's protracted growing:*
> *June rear'd that bunch of flowers you carry,*
> *From seeds of April's sowing.*
>
> ~*~
>
> *I plant a heartful now: some seed*
> *At least is sure to strike,*
> *And yield—what you'll not pluck indeed,*
> *Not love, but, may be, like.*
>
> ~*~
>
> *You'll look at least on love's remains,*
> *A grave's one violet:*
> *Your look?—that pays a thousand pains.*
> *What's death? You'll love me yet!*
>
> ~Robert Browning

And once the words were spoken, she had the inner strength to make this dream become reality. Holding the flute at a slight angle by his mouth, she let a few drops land on his tongue and watched to see if his throat would move on its own. It didn't. So she poured a few more, and then held his mouth shut. He still didn't move on his own or even become startled enough to sit up. Her anger was a riot inside her previously settled mind at how the pieces were falling apart at the seams. Steeling herself, she poured the goop into his mouth and then took my other pillow to position it over his face. She would practically suffocate him with the pillow to get the effect she hoped for. Just as I feared for his immediate safety, he jerked about under the stuffed offender. Yanking the pillow off, his throat began working. I'd heard the trick done to animals who wouldn't swallow pills and it was a certainty that she knew none of the newest methods of emergency care. I imagine worst procedures had been used a hundred years ago.

His throat bobbed again and his lips worked as he began to take in the consistency of what was being administered to him. A hand came up to wipe a sliver of dribble running down his strong chin. I waited for him to open those lovely eyes but they remained shut. Was his body automatically taking care of him or could his subconscious be trying to wake him from this horrible situation? Maybe he was faking it so she would leave him to devise a plan. If the later was the case then it would all be in vain if he woke to a love so deep where his thoughts were drowned in the sorrowful depths.

Chapter Sixteen

Kenrick didn't open his mesmerizing eyes after taking in the full portion of the potion. I had hoped he would jump up, spit the gruesome remains into her pale face, and declare his feelings for me. All I got instead was a self-satisfied feeling spewed from the witch who had taken over my form. I was appalled that she may well have everything she came back to life for. Maybe if I could get my hands on her diary, then I could see if there was a way to reverse it or even something in there to destroy her life force altogether. But to do that, I would have to make her take me.

Then it hit me. If I was lucky enough to somehow get what I needed through Kenrick, then I could see if he could devise the required items to survive this. He possessed more knowledge about her than I did. This would only work if he woke up as himself and not her love puppet. I doubted I was crafty enough to trick him into finding something to destroy the link she fought to create with him. My only solution was to see what happened when he woke up and joined us in this play for life.

Resting up throughout the remainder of the day, I didn't force my way into any visuals or sounds from my captor. My thoughts plotted every scenario pertaining to me or Kenrick. No matter what I could devise, it seemed that I was bound by knowing whether Kenrick would be with me or against me. One good question was if Kenrick woke a lovesick slave, would he still be able to visit ladies in their dreams? I hadn't seen anything that led to my particular curse being removed. She wouldn't need him to love her body and then again love her in her state of REM sleep. It might empower him but I didn't see her allowing him to gain enough strength from her if it cost her some of her witch powers. Would I be able to call on him in that manner, instead of him just invading my mind?

At dinner, she sat at the small table with a single taper candle in front of her china plate. She relished the flavors of the poached eggs and steamed salmon for her meal. I never liked the stuff so I was glad I didn't have to share the taste of it. It seemed even more of an assault on my freedom as she delighted in one of her favorite meals from days gone by. After she finished the disgusting meal, she washed the dishes in the sink and exuded her happiness on me. If only I could shut her completely out, maybe I would be able to keep my sanity about me for a few years longer. Trying to stay numb, it would cut to the core every time she forced her happiness on me, at the expense of my mortal life.

She waltzed up the staircase in the dark and pushed her feelings of eagerness upon me. Gloating was never a becoming trait and I wanted to use the small amount of power I had salvaged to expel her from me at that very moment. If I couldn't make her leave my body then I could at least not have to feel what she chose to feed me in this sick game. Just as I was about to give a huge mental push, I caught a flicker in her thoughts. She wanted me to do this. Her game plan relied on me expending what little I had not used to keep me from having any sexual encounters with Kenrick once she fell asleep in my bed. The bitch was ruthless. Fighting my large stubborn streak, I let her rain all over my raw feelings.

Once in my room, she strode over to the gilded mirror by the small closet and slowly stripped off my clothing. She looked over every inch of my freckled skin to see what she liked and disliked about her new form. It was degrading as she ran her hand over my small perky breasts, wishing she still had her more rounded ones. The flat plain of my stomach made her feel better as she had hated that part of her old body. My hips weren't as full as hers had been, but she would be okay with them as my legs were strong and muscular. Making a face of disdain at the clothing on the floor, she knew one of the first things she would do was go shopping with her new bank account. She had never been able to do it before and didn't like the drab colors of my worn attire but she had no choice since my previous meager budget could only purchase so much. Soon she would own flowing dresses and sexy nightgowns of silk and satin.

A shudder of anticipation escaped her as she shifted under the sheets, and the weight of the man on the bed had her in a more intimate hold than she was used to. Last night, exhaustion had taken away the sparkling newness of her being in bed with a man. Tonight, she had goosebumps as she told herself that she would have more than just a subtle embrace to warm her through the blustery night. If I could vomit, I would have. Having sex in my mind was bearable but her having it with a real man in my body was just twenty shades of wrong.

Sleep claimed her before I could try to prevent anything from happening to my unprotected anatomy. But the dream that captured us was unlike any I had experienced. Maybe the combined power of the three people involved caused this but I wasn't expecting what I saw. I was looking at Aster's ghost form as she became more dense and unghost like. We were in the yard halfway between the house and the greenhouse. I recognized the tree she used to stand under when watching him work with the delicate plants.

After taking a hesitant step, she left the tree behind, and I saw her stealthily move toward the greenhouse. She would keep peeking into the doors to see if anything would be made clear to her before she got to the threshold. I didn't get the sense that she had any clue but she went along with her dream, hoping it would still end in the same amount of sexual bliss. I was not a part of her as she moved along in this scene. I wasn't looking down at her either, as any type of ethereal or metaphysical being. This confirmed my thought as she looked straight at me before she got two steps away from the door left ajar. I knew she was glaring at me, in some type of question as to whether she should move forward or should I. If this ride belonged to her then I would remain still and wait to see what the cards had in store for us.

Her confusion over us both being there was written on her alabaster skinned face. She had to have mistakenly taken me along for the journey or Kenrick had plans for both of us. We would soon find out which way this path would unwind. After she finally made herself go into the greenhouse, I followed a few paces behind her. I almost ran into her as soon as I cleared the glass door. She stared longingly at Kenrick who was clipping buds off of a small plant that had not been in any of my other visions. The arrays of plants were a mixture of old and new as both worlds were combined. Some of the older items held a more sepia tone, as if from a vintage photograph.

Kenrick wore a dark green button up cotton shirt with rolled up sleeves that flapped about his jeans pockets since it was untucked. The denim encasing his legs seemed heavier and a darker wash than we had in the modern time. It felt like an odd combination but he carried it off with confidence. Picking up a different plant, he carried it to the shelf that Aster used to use for her diary and potion making. There were only a couple of things there and none of them felt as if they were hers. This was Kenrick's doing and he showed his control over this scene.

Looking at both of us, he made a gentle shrugging motion for us to come closer. We obliged but I wasn't too sure where to stand in this situation, figuratively and literally. Staying in the back corner, by the still open door, I waited to see what this was all about. Aster, being bolder, walked along the three rows of plants to see what had been called forth. Gingerly, she touched a few and even stuck a fingertip in the soil of one plant to check the moisture of the potting mixture. Then she made her way to Kenrick, with a sway to her fuller hips under the almost transparent gauze of her white dress. If I didn't dislike her so much, I would say that she was a seductive picture with the light pinpointing areas of her curved frame as she made her intentions known.

Once within reach of her target, she spoke, "You

called and we are here."

"Yes, I did."

The next moment he had her wrapped in his arms in a hold more aggression than carnal. Her back was roughly against his chest with one of his sleeved arms just at her breastbone. I wasn't sure if he meant to choke her or to simply hold her as he said what he needed to say. In no way would I help her as she remained the villain here, even if my natural instinct was to save a woman in possible danger.

"What shall I ever do with you my dear wicked witch?" he asked in a low enough voice that seemed to be more for the delicate ear just below his parted mouth.

"That would depend entirely on what you have in mind, sir," she suggestively replied.

He turned to me. "I have a few ideas running around my head but I'm not sure how well they would be received by Renata?"

"You know how I feel, Kenrick, so there is nothing to discuss further on that matter," I simply stated.

"Then I guess it's up to me to make the next move on this chess board," he said with a small sigh.

"Chess only has two players, my dear," retorted Aster.

"That it does, dear witch. That it does."

A scream of terror escaped me as I was tossed against the glass wall behind me and the door swung with a force that jolted me between the cold wall and the unwavering glass door. My arms were pinned to my sides between those two chilly surfaces and I barely had enough room to lift my fingers as I tried in vain to push it away from me. My small nose was pressed so close to the glass my heavy breathing fogged up the images in front of me. I began to panic. Could I hyperventilate in a dream? Did our combined power have enough strength to actually kill me, as old wives tales once deemed to be true?

Hearing distorted laughter, I knew with renewed dread that I had been betrayed. He may not have woken to make love to her in body but he had enough of the heinous potion in him to have him with her as they slept together in my bed. Railing against my dangerous cell, I almost forgot the chance that my struggles could shatter the materials embracing me. What would be worse? Seeing them as I made myself pass out? Making enough of a ruckus where I broke the walls around me, possibly causing myself dangerous injuries? Using what little amount of power I had stored to force myself out of this dream and into the gray mind of the woman who continued to possess my body?

As the fog began to dissipate, I saw something best left unseen. The embrace that had started as defensive notched up to a sexual heat as he had pulled Aster into a kiss too hot for any simple display of affection. This was the type of memory that lovers took pride creating when separated from each other for too long of a time. Not for a couple sworn to torment each other for a hundred years. Feeling my heart sink like a lead weight in the ocean, I saw how hands roved over each other's bodies like they were memorizing the acute grooves in a marble statue. Roughly, she began to disconnect the buttons on his shirt and get his skin under her greedy hands. He made no move to stop her, the lecher. As a matter of fact, he had leaned away from her in an attempt to give her hands more room to maneuver.

His shirt flew to the ground in a fluttering heap and she began running her lips over the skin so nicely exposed to her. A warm chuckle trickled from his chest as her head moved around to take in as many inches as possible of his lightly sculpted torso. Even though I was smothered, I could make out the noise of panting and light moans coming from them. Disgusted, I closed my eyes when he bent down to pull the white cotton dress over her trim shoulders. More of her hated laughter rang into the metal rafters as I squeezed my eyes shut so tightly spots danced before my eyelids. A sexy groan assaulted my ears and I heard a thump as something heavy hit the floor and rattled the door. Opening my eyes to hopefully see her immobile on the ground, I gasped when I realized what was truly happening not a few feet from me.

There they were, both stark naked, and rolling around the debris-strewn wood below us. Bile rose in my constricted throat as I saw him pose above her. I couldn't take it. I couldn't fathom sitting here as they made love in front of me. It wasn't just my more humble sensibilities but the moral wrongness of the situation which had me shoving against the now heated glass while I screamed to be released. It that moment they stopped and looked at me, with her face mid-gasp and his hovering above her breast.

"No!"

I launched my body and my force against the vibrating barrier and with a cry from my fractured heart, the glass hurtled away from me in a million pieces of rage. It showered them as it ripped across delicate skin. Coming away from the wall that had remained solid in my actions, I stalked over to the pair stuttering up at me.

The shaking limbs of the witch were riddled in glass fragments and blood welled from her many cuts and scrapes. I gazed upon my deceitful lover and was in a moment of shock as he pulled a small dagger of glass from the arm he had held up to protect his gorgeous face. Laying the glass at his hip, he surveyed the wound that needed stitches if inflicted upon real flesh. My mind had a hard time accepting it wasn't actual blood flowing down to drip across the uncovered skin of Aster's rounded belly. A pool of red had already collected in her small navel, looking macabre in its gleam across her chalky white complexion.

Blinking as he began to move under the assault of my eyes, he reached for his shirt, ripping a sleeve off to wrap around his lower arm as a makeshift bandage and tourniquet. Quickly the green turned to a mottled brown as the cotton drank in the red blood oozed from his wound. Again, it seemed so realistic that I had to remind myself of the fact we all were wrapped in this dream.

As my attention was drawn back to Aster, she had a wondrous gleam in her bedeviled eyes. How could she seem so satisfied when I had stopped her being ravaged by my betraying lover? She should be angry that I had not only stopped her plan of seduction but he had been left to bleed as he tried to keep his face from being damaged. Flicking my glance to Kenrick, my eyes begged the question as words were not available to me. His uninjured hand went from under Aster's head to point at my right side.

That's the moment I felt the searing pain as I took in the view of a large shard of jagged green glass embedded in my tender flesh. I hadn't even known I was injured. Was it the dream world keeping me safe inside my own head or was it that my mind hadn't accepted the damage I had done? If I survived this, I would know whether dreams had the ability to influence the flesh. Knowing you should never pull out an item impaling you, I painfully reached for his tattered shirt and yanked the remaining sleeve free from the shoulder seam. As quickly as possible I would pluck the shard from my upper hip and stuff the wad of cotton in the hole to use as a compression bandage.

Just when I gathered the strength to grasp the jagged edge, Aster was on her feet and in my personal space. Kenrick's voice interrupted the tense air as I prepared to lunge away from her.

"Let me take care of this, my Aster," he said strongly enough to grab both our attentions.

"Do you have the will to take care of it completely?"

Such an odd question for her to ask as dark red bloomed across my stomach.

He began to walk forward but she put a blood sprinkled hand up to stop him before reaching me.

"I demand an answer to my question, besotted one."

She wanted to know if he could kill me. *Shit!*

With them decently distracted, I lurched to the left to escape both sets of hands, and the plans they had for me. Hearing a cry of frustration from Aster, I tried to move my legs faster as blood loss was becoming more evident with my stilted actions. A rush of wind ran across me as a large shadow quickly loomed over my retreating figure. I could see it like a harbinger of death as it swallowed up my shadow by the time I reached the broken door frame. It beat upon me before I could save myself. I was flung to the ground just outside the greenhouse, on the stone pathway leading me back to the house.

Using my hands to keep myself from falling flat on my face and impaling myself to dangerous degrees, the force had me in so much pain that I fought off fear I would vomit if I moved too quickly. But this was just a dream, right? Could I force my mind to conquer my imagination and the intent of a witch? Slowly getting to all fours, I was too late as I heard them slowly walk up behind me. Just as I put more effort into standing, although not as straight as before, Kenrick steadied me by holding my left elbow in his tight grip.

"Move away from her unless you have the balls to finish this," Aster ground out.

"Back off, Aster. I know what I'm doing," he said to her as he looked into my frightened eyes.

"I want the pleasure of running this little rabbit through."

She sounded pleased with his phrasing in pursuing her fiendish plan. If he wasn't going to do it then she would and neither one of them seemed to want it any other way.

"If you're going to kill me then get it the fuck over with. I'm tired of this madness and you can have each other. Just let me go to heaven and be done with this," I exclaimed with my slurring words of pain and bloodshed.

"Aww, the rabbit wants to be freed. We can take care of that little detail for you, Ms. Renata Barkely," came Aster's acidic voice.

My fatigue was overwhelming. My muscles didn't want to hold me up for much longer. In this nightmare, I was bleeding to death while they bickered over who was going to cast the fatal blow. A hysterical chortle escaped my dry throat, and I clutched at Kenrick.

Aster popped her head up around the arms that held me. "Either way, there will be a death this evening, and we're wasting valuable time, my love."

"You're right, Aster, this has gone on long enough," came from the betraying lips of the man I loved.

Chapter Seventeen

His eyes flashed like flame to a new log and I remembered his eyes erupting with passion for me. It had been real, no matter what he may feel for Aster at the moment. I felt, more than saw, his lean fingers slide over the blood coated glass and pull it out with a deft motion that wrenched my insides. Surprise ran across me as I had somehow hoped he wouldn't do such a thing after saying he wanted to court me.

I said the only words available to my fleeting mind, "No matter what happens, just know that I love you, Kenrick Giles."

Aster roared with laughter at not only my words but at the fact that my words ended in symmetry to him ending my life.

"How quaint. Now drop the foolish woman and take me to bed, my long lost lover," Aster said as she pushed me from his arms and to the ground.

They just stood over me, watching the sea of red wrapping itself around me like wet silk. I wanted his eyes to be the last thing I saw, but just as I willed them to shut forever, he did something else to surprise us all. Taking the glass still in his grip, he turned and thrust it into the breast of the witch at his side.

An inhuman bellow emitted from her parted lips and my ears rang with the force of it. Kenrick slammed down beside me as curls of black smoke shot out of the hole in the witch's naked chest. Red flames sparked and licked at her feet, and Kenrick scooped me up and away before they caught onto my blood-soaked clothing. Sadly, the black enveloped us before he could get me safely away from my would-be murderer.

****

Popping my eyes open, I saw sage green and cream designs across the walls of my bedroom. Then Kenrick's face came into view and I swallowed the scream that crawled up from my lungs. Trying to edge further from him, a pain shot through me and took my breath away from me.

"Be still, the wound needs to be packed," said the man with the eyes of burning topaz stone.

"Oh my God, the fucking wound is real. You son of a bitch!"

"I'm sorry this had to happen but it was the only way," he said as he yanked a pillow from the floor and struggled to get the cotton casing off. He shook so badly he had too tight of a grip on the pillow to properly get the fabric off, but he wasn't going to drop it and get more debris on it. He was dressed in the jeans and shirt from his dream including the stained remnant around his arm.

"Why?" I managed to squeeze out from clenched teeth as I prepared myself for the coming procedure.

"I've seen the book and there were only a few things possible to dispel her from you. Most were more dangerous than this and I panicked. I knew she was going to kill you in the dream. I couldn't let that happen. The initial wound was extreme enough but your falling made everything worse."

As he packed the wad into my gaping wound, I let

the hysteria seep out of me with a scream which sounded like the wounded animal I was.

"So, this is my fault?" bubbled out of me in an angry sob.

He paused for a moment before looking at me with a smirk on his face.

"Yes, all of this is your doing as you are too delicious a meal for us old fogeys."

If I'd had the strength then I would have laughed or smacked him. Both were still up for debate.

"We have to stop the blood flow as we try to get out of here," he said to me as he got a majority of the wound filled with cloth.

"You and I both know she's not going to just let us go. That witch is too vain to be ignored, and she's going to take us out if she can't have her way with us," I said around gasps while he worked at staunching the blood.

I had to ask, to know, even if he lied through his straight teeth. "Why are you trying to save me when you were just seducing *her*? You had said you wanted to court me and then you went with *her*. Was it the drugs and if so, how did you overcome them? If you were trying to get close to *her* then you went way overboard with your acting, man."

"You're right but I was pushing off the remnants of what I had ingested while remaining in control of the dream we were spinning. I had held as much as I could in my mouth without swallowing it but some of it got down my throat when she covered my face. I fought not to gag as I knew she would have a tiny bit of control over me, even if I didn't fall in love with her. Maybe my curse deflected the potion. Whatever it was, thank the gods."

"I personally would have thrown up, and I don't see how you laid there so peacefully while she did that to you. But then again, you ended up naked and writhing against her well enough. If I'm to trust you then how do I know what is make-believe from real feelings? I can't just turn to blind faith after the stunt you just pulled, potion or not."

"All I can say is that I'm sorry for hurting you. It wasn't my intention, and there was no way I would have intercourse with that creature. Don't even waste the energy on it. But I had to make it look real to fool her. You saw it with your own eyes and believed it."

"You were leaving me to bleed to death!" I choked out as a wave of pain at his last adjustment had my spine bowing.

"It was the only way to force her out of you. I swear. And I plan on making this up to you, if you'll let me."

"I seriously can't see you being trustworthy anymore."

He looked defeated as the heated words sank into him. Wiping his hands on a cloth, he wouldn't meet my eyes. Why did I have to feel guilty after the stunt he had pulled on me? This was insane!

Before I could stop the words, I said, "If we get out of this alive, then I'll let you explain how you think you can make me trust you again."

"When. Not if. And you have yourself a deal, Miss Barkley."

I took a few deep breaths as I forced myself to sit up.

"We need to find her diary and burn the damned

thing to ashes. Do you think you can come with me? I'm afraid to leave you alone and vulnerable in case she can somehow get back into you in your weakened condition."

"If waiting for her to assault me is the option then I'd rather be running with you," I stated honestly. I knew that I had lost too much blood but there was no way in hell I would just lay around and wait for her to go back to wherever she flew in from.

"It's a start," he replied as he held his hand out for me to take.

Hesitating for a fraction of a minute, I gripped his hand as he pulled me to the hallway and then down the stairs to the front foyer.

"We both have a link to her, so we need to think of where the book might be hidden. The real one wasn't in her dream, just a manufactured one. I'd bet she doesn't need the book to make the potion since she's had almost a century to memorize the damned thing while she grew stronger."

"If I had to guess, I'd say the attic, the library, the greenhouse, or the cemetery."

They were the only plausible places in this maddening scenario.

"What do you think, Kenrick?"

"I agree with the attic and the library but not the other two. Those last two would involve her burying them in the ground and that leather isn't going to handle soil very well, or the old pages inside of it."

"We're running out of time, so we either start checking every piece of the estate or we concentrate the effort on only the most likely of places."

"You're right, but I don't want to split up since

we're easier prey alone."

"Fine. Let's go to the attic first, then the library on the way back down."

And we were at it. Well, as quickly as my wound would allow us. At one point, I shifted the bandage a little as to not show that the blood had already soaked the area showing. Something had to be done since I could not simply lie down like a victim and take this. Unfortunately, there was no book, or any of her items, left in the attic and no sign of anything in the library.

"You know you've lost your chance of being uncursed after you banished her out of me, right?" I asked as we made our way to the front door. But one of my legs wavered on the second to bottom step, spilling me to the wooden floor like a rag doll.

This was the worst possible moment to have my next vision. It seeped into my mind like the blood that trickled into the grooves of the polished wood flooring. I wondered if I was dying as I saw myself in a growing puddle and tangled limbs. Feeling as if a magnet had been placed inside of my floating transparent body, I was slowly drawn away from the distraught look on Kenrick's face as he tried to wake me up. Thankfully, the attempt wasn't working as I shifted to the kitchen, hearing a hum coming from the drafty door in the kitchen. It shifted from being a pull at my center to a cold gust which blew my thoughts around as I focused on what could be causing this to happen.

I heard Kenrick yell, "Come back to me, Renata. Please don't leave me. We were so close to finishing this shit. Just come back and I swear to fix everything."

It nearly broke my heart to hear the desperation in his hoarse voice. Was he crying? If my body was dying then the bitch couldn't have it anymore. I could accept that fact but I didn't want to leave the chance I had for a new life. Reaching for the door, my hand went through the knob in a blinding speed. *Shit.* Don't let me be dead. I had to help Kenrick. If I couldn't be used then Aster would find a way to still get back at Kenrick, even if it meant possessing a body long enough to kill him. I knew it.

The air still yanked at me like wind pulling at a lonely kite. Saying a prayer, I let it take me and when it did I suddenly found myself on the other side of the wooden door and shooting down the eerie darkness of the tunnel. My speed kept me from knowing how far down I had gone and I wondered if I would appear on the other side of the field in a flash of color and speed. No, I was stopped with a sudden force and aimed at the cold stone wall. Why? Not being able to move forward or backward, I turned and examined the wall itself. There. A small crevice was evident near the floor and I bent down to it since I had been allowed more movement by my metaphysical bonds. I had to be close to something important because the energy was concentrated in this one specific spot.

My hands disappeared into the porous surface of the concrete wall and swept around as I fought to see what was hidden there. After several attempts and nothing, I did the unthinkable and jammed my head just above the indention in the wall. The humming came back and rang so loudly that my head ached with it. How could it even be possible? Then I realized the noise was coming from the leather-bound book hidden inside the wall for safe keeping. I bet she hadn't ever guessed I'd be able to find it here.

Just as I put energy into reaching for it, a throbbing focus at my fingers become more dense, I felt the wind pulling me back out of the wall. *No!* I had to get the book for Kenrick. Grabbing for purchase anywhere, I was helpless against stopping the suction as I was being evicted from the hallway and hauled back into the kitchen. The door slammed against the frame in the supernatural force that zapped me back into the bleeding body under Kenrick's life-saving lips.

Eyes aching and lungs heaving, I spasmed after my spirit was forced into my frame worse than a head-on collision. His hands were still on my chest, where he'd been performing CPR on me. No wonder they hurt like hell.

"Book. Escape hall. Kitchen."

That was all I could choke out as he put pressure on my hip wound again.

"It stopped bleeding. What did you do?"

"Get the book!" I croaked out as I pointed in the general direction of where my spirit had found the witch diary. "Now! No time!"

He must have believed me because he ran straight to the kitchen and skidded to a stop at the passageway door. I heard the slam as it ricocheted against the wall and then nothing as he raced down. *Shit.* I hadn't told him how far down it was or what to look for. He'd never find it. Using my hands as best as I could, I wrenched my body up as I held tightly to a spindle on the stair banister. Trying to yell at him, it wasn't audible to my own ears, let alone his as he ran down the dark tunnel. Half limping and half yanking myself from one sturdy piece of furniture to the next, I ran out of things to cling to once I got over the threshold to the kitchen. Gathering all of the air I could in my tortured lungs, I screamed, "Halfway down. Floor crevice. Right side. Focus on your curse!" And then I let myself hit the floor as my strength refused to hold my weight any longer.

Lying there, I felt no discomfort, which was odd when you're a mass of bones on a cold wooden floor. Shouldn't I be feeling more pain with that jolt? Did I care as long as he found the damned book and beat Aster to death with it? No. Not really.

Blackness grew larger and larger in my view as oblivion asked to claim me for its own. I teetered on the verge of accepting when I heard a woot of happiness from Kenrick and then stomping as he came back to me. Trying to smile, I touched at the blackness weighing heavily on me but it was flung away as my lover scooped me up into his warm embrace. I held onto my narrow ray of hope.

"No. I didn't get this far to see you slipping away. You're no slug, lady."

I would have laughed if I could have gotten it out of my lungs. Eyelashes fluttering, I heard him rummaging through the musty pages of the despicable book.

"There has to be something here. She had too many tricks to not have one for this kind of thing. Where the hell is it?"

Flip flip flip went the stiff pages. It sounded like the wings of a black swan coming to carry me away.

"Hold on, damn it! Fuck, here it is." He sounded so frightened but nothing would ever be as scary as Aster the reborn witch.

Latin words spilled from him as he held me close

to his chest. Sounding like a heady mix of sexual innuendo and guttural language, they wove around me as I didn't want to fight anymore. Muscle cramps of monster proportion sank into me like shark teeth. Going rigid, he held me as if I might possibly disintegrate. Screaming as if it was the last thing that I would ever accomplish, it all went away as the air heaved out of me. Gasping, my eyes popped open to look up at the burning topaz of the man who had just spelled me back to a better state of health. Frantically, I swept away the ragged fabric at my hip and saw the skin scabbed over and looking more like a nasty scratch than any stab wound should ever appear.

"You saved my life," was the first thing uttered from my lips. At least it wasn't the word golly.

"We're not out of the woods yet. Can you manage to get up?" he asked as he slowly straightened up.

"Let's go kick some witchy ass."

Hand in hand, we ran for the cemetery as he had the diary under his left arm. Once we passed the greenhouse, the pressure changed and my ears popped as an unholy cry broke along the tree line. This was no storm-riddled wind. This embodied the rage of a witch powered ghost who had found a way to come back at us.

"Run and don't look back!" Kenrick yelled to me over the roar around us.

The ground shifted apart, we had to jump over the cracks that ripped at the grass in front of us and the shifting walls of the greenhouse shattered like a mirror in a bonfire. It felt like ant bites along my exposed skin as tiny fragments of glass flew around us in a whirlwind of bloodletting. My feet were a mass of wounds as we scampered across the debris-covered ground to the crest before the weeping willow tree. Jolts of adrenaline kept me from skidding across the rocky wall as I flung myself over the barrier and behind its low protection.

"Can we make it to her plot?" I asked him as we caught our breath.

"We're going to have to. On the count of three…" And we were off, battling the wind.

He led me to where her tombstone stood and we fell to our knees as the wind buffeted around us and he fumbled around in his pocket.

"What are you doing?" I screamed at him.

Then Aster appeared on top of him and the book of matches flew from his hands. Slamming him into the trunk of the willow, leaves shook down with the impact of his body hitting it.

"You dared to stab me? You loathsome cur!"

Frantically, I fumbled around for the damned book as the grass bobbed around it in the wind from Aster. Taking several tries to keep it in my grip, I saw there were only two matches left in the tatty matchbook. I only had two chances to burn this book and I didn't think she'd be gracious enough to stop the wind so I could melt that book into fucking ashes.

Kenrick howled as she kept smacking his head into the wood of the tree. Just as she was about to toss him at me, I struck the match and held it to the center of the book pages. Smoke began to rise and Aster hurled him like a bowling ball right at me. When we struck, my teeth jarred and my leg went out from under me in a sickening crunch. Kenrick had blood seeping from the back of his head and a collar of red slid around his strong neck. It was about to get nasty. I had to console myself with the image of his chest taking in air.

Aster was a purple and black cloud of menace above us as her hands began moving in a graceful dance and Latin wove out of her lips. She was either going to blast us to hell or toss a curse of satanic proportion down on us. The stirrings of it hit and electricity branched across the sky. Then I realized I was laying on the diary and the last match.

"Kenrick, do you hear me?"

"Mmmm," was all he managed.

"Can you try to distract her?"

He went to nod but then grabbed at his injured throat. I knew he understood me. Gripping a handful of tall weeds, he pulled himself away from me. I stayed as still as possible so she remained focused on him and not my actions.

"Hey, bitchy witch, looking for me?"

The words were the wrong thing to say as she flung a bolt of energy into his chest. Hating the amount of pain he had to be in, I still had to destroy her. So I edged the lone match up and struck it under my lowered chest. It took flame and began to burn at my skin as I set it upon the dried-out pages of the dreaded book. Tears streamed down my face as a ragged cry came from Kenrick and I heard him slump to the ground. But the pages were lit and I wasn't going to release it unless it planned to take me with it. Even that was debatable. The flame wicked enough to catch onto my shirt and I had to tear it over my head as I struggled to turn over onto the grave under me.

The leather in my hands began to warp under the searing flames and spread at too slow a pace for my liking. I didn't have time for this. Aster emitted her hideous laugh and called out to me. I wouldn't look at her for fear she could somehow bespell me. I wasn't dying anymore so she had to have a backup plan for possessing me. She hadn't survived a century of time without having some of it spent on ways to keep her spirit alive. Just as she reached those dead hands out to me, I slammed the burning book against the desecrated name on the tombstone and held it there for all I was worth. Red hot nails dug across my back and buttocks as she tried to yank me away from her place of power.

Smoke curled in a tail of a wisp up from the stone and Aster stabbed her nails into my hips as she screamed the world down around us. Branches were jagged splinters, stones were bullets against my human skin. The wrath of a ghost scorned rained upon me and then I saw nothing. Felt nothing. I said goodbye and prayed my love weathered the storm.

Chapter Eighteen

A soft white glow greeted me and I sighed heavily as the scent of gardenias filled the air.

"She's coming to, Mr. Giles," said an unrecognizable female voice above me.

My eyes were so heavy it took effort to make them open but I had to see who was in my room. The feminine voice belonged to an older lady with silver threaded hair and she had a tablet in front of her.

"Who are you and where am I?" I whispered to her.

"I'm Nurse Ann and I'm going to go let the doctor know that you opened those pretty eyes. I'll be right back," she said and closed the door behind her. I deduced that I had been admitted to a hospital, but she hadn't said which one.

"I'm glad to see you've joined the living again," said a familiar masculine voice from the right side of my bed.

"Have I?" came the best humor in me at that moment.

"Yes, it was touch and go a few times but you're too stubborn to be anything but extraordinary." He knelt by the side of the bed.

I began to reach for the tray on the other side of the bed and realized I was sore in too many places to count. There appeared to be a heavy bandage around my throbbing hand. Then I remembered not only the slice in his palm but the book burning as the world had cracked open around me.

"Aster! What happened to her? Oh God, is she going to come after us?"

He pushed me back into the pillows. "Shh, it's taken care of."

"Tell me what happened," I said to him as I waited impatiently for the words I needed to hear.

"What do you remember?"

I relayed the images, even of him being slammed into the tree plus him getting the attention off of me as I set the last match to the pages of the book.

"I'm sorry you got hurt because of me. How are you?" I asked as he slipped the cup of ice chips to my uninjured hand.

The cold felt good against my desert-dry mouth, and I let a few pieces melt on my tongue as I waited for him to respond.

"How about we make a deal? You forgive me for killing the taste buds off of my tongue faking that witch out and I'll forgive you for throwing me to her tender attention so you could burn yourself up like a hot dog," he said as he put a hand out for me to shake.

"I like how you put it but I have a hard time getting that image fried from my cells," I said as I ignored his hand.

"Then I have a lot of work ahead of me as I beg you to forgive me. But can you at least be satisfied it happened in a dream and not in the flesh?"

He had a good point, so I said, "I'll give you a few years to persuade me to trust you again, slut."

As he looked at me in shock, I started to giggle but then noticed my chest aching beyond the confines of the pain medication. Leaning back against the institutional pillows, I relaxed so the pain would subside a bit. When it did, Kenrick was looking at me with a pleased expression on his face. His neck had turned a nice shade of dusty eggplant as it showed the print of the fingers that had tried to choke the life out of my lover. I'm glad he didn't let it happen.

"I'll give you a few years, if it's what you want," he questioned with a sexy look in those eyes.

"Fine, three years tops."

"We can seal it with a kiss, right? I am still Cajun." He used his old line on me again.

He was bold in asking but I had to be worse for wanting it. Not turning him down, he took it for an acceptance. His warm lips were on mine and I closed my eyes as I felt him lick the edge of my top lip. Just when I thought he would deepen the kiss, he pulled back. The look on his face kept me from complaining as I saw raw need in his gaze.

"Going gentle on me, old man?" I asked.

"No, ma'am. I'm just saving it up for a rainy day."

That made me think of the rain we kept having at the house but in a good way.

"So, fill me in on the rest of what happened plus go over my injuries. I know there is a list, so you can just get it all over with in one big breath."

"You have a burned hand from holding the flaming book to the headstone for so long that we almost had to pry you from it. You already had the healing hip, which I couldn't explain to the doctors, several cuts from all of the shrapnel you went through at the cemetery, plus a random assortment of claw marks across your backside. That gave you a total of three which are glued shut and two having thirteen stitches all total for both of those being closed up. The worst of it is the broken leg from when she catapulted me onto you."

"Shit. How'd the other gal look?" I joked.

"She had some psychic chick hold her soul to a burning stone and got busted into a bazillion little pieces of mummified corpse."

Softly chuckling came from me. "No way. She was a ghost and they don't do that."

"I exaggerated. But her soul did explode and there's no way to come back from having your essence splashed across three properties."

Ick.

"Are you sure she can't come back? And she can't try to possess me again?"

"Let's just say that I did a little undercover work while they set your leg, and you're safe from the old bitty. The bad news is you accidentally absorbed all of her power away from her before you shoved it into the grave dust where she belonged."

"I'm glad I did something right. It's a shame she couldn't have taken your curse with her. Well, if you still have it," I hedged.

"Sadly, I still have it," he answered.

"What are you going to do about it?" I swallowed my fear to ask but it added up to nothing compared to what I'd been through already.

"There's this girl I know that really enjoys naps. Maybe I can convince her to help me out until I find someone who can counter curse me," he mentioned as he looked at the door.

"No fucking way!"

He laughed and it was wonderful to hear. "Hun,

I'm talking about you."

I had to have turned four shades of red, realizing he was pulling my broken leg. If I hadn't been so tired, I would have thrown my pillow at his mocking face.

"I'm going to kick your ass when we get out of here." I pointed an unbandaged finger at him.

"I'm looking forward to it." He saluted me and I smiled.

Maybe this would be fine. Who knew?

The next day the doctor discharged me from the hospital which happened to be an hour away from the estate. On the way home, we'd talked about a few loose ends that had to be handled around the house. The greenhouse barely had anything left to it except the metal frame but it was intact enough to get the glass replaced if we wanted to set it back up again. The willow tree had been split in half by Aster's rain of lightning so we weren't sure if it would survive another year. If it died, then I'd plant a magnolia tree in its place. Mr. White had already sent a construction worker to replace the window in my room and had tidied up the mess we made around the house in our mad dashes for safety. Not once was he given an answer for what had actually happened to cause so much damage. Sadly, with us being in the hospital, he probably thought we had beaten each other up in a lover's quarrel. I would have to be okay with letting him believe that. I just wanted to be safe in my own home for a while. It was the most important thing to me right now. Well, the sexy man who happened to be helping me out of the car stood a very close second.

"I hope you aren't mad at me for turning in the papers Aster signed," Kenrick said as he set my crutches against the passenger side of the car my grandfather had left at the back of the property. "It was still your hand that signed them and she invariably did what you wanted, so I didn't feel he needed to know the scenario of how your signature had gotten on the paperwork."

Pulling me gently from the passenger seat, I let him linger with his arms around me. "I had already decided to stay and even though it bugs me how it happened, it was what was meant to be either way."

"Good. It's one less thing for you to hold against me." He ticked off a point in the air between us and grinned at me.

Gently smacking his shoulder, I let him laugh at my expense.

A squeal popped out of me when he swung me up into his arms and nudged the door shut with a booted foot. The keys to the house were in one of the hands that held me soundly against his warm chest. With a flick of his deft fingers, the keys skimmed down my breasts and pooled in my lap as he walked a few more steps to the front door.

"Would you please do the honors, my dear damsel in distress?"

Shaking my head at him, I smiled and held the keys so I could insert them once he had me in arm's length of the front door. A dirty joke or two was mentioned as I fumbled my way to having the lock handled but it was all in good humor. Once inside, he set me on the closest seat of the couch in the foyer, leaning me against the tapestry pillows.

"As your room is on the second floor and the kitchen and laundry are down here, where would you like to sleep for the next few hours?"

"It's not bedtime yet," I reminded him.

"Right now it's about to chime four o'clock and you are tired from escaping an awful room of antiseptic and overprotective nurses."

"Yes, but I'd like to sleep this evening. If I have insomnia after the recent events, you'll have to put up with a worse female than Aster," I joked as it was the only way to make the horrid events easier to get through.

"You're that kind of cranky after lack of sleep? Goodness, then you really are a lady after my own heart as I adore a woman who knows how to appreciate a glorious amount of sleep."

The sly look slid back into his eyes and my heart thrilled at the possibilities.

"This is padded enough that I can rest here," I decided. Even if it was a sexily romantic idea, I was not about to have him carrying me up and down a flight of stairs because I was selfish enough to want the comfort of the bed my body had just gotten used to up there. He headed back out for my bag and crutches when I closed my eyes and thought over how comfortable I felt at this moment. It wasn't just the furnishings my grandmother had lovingly picked out but a presence that encompassed the whole house. Not only had I fallen in love with a handsome caretaker but the house we were to live in. Together. I'd only had a few roommates and they were all girls in the dorm rooms, so this had evolved itself into a whole new world for me as I took over the reins on what needed to be done to make this place prosper.

Kenrick and I were still debating what to do with

the greenhouse. We'd have to talk to Mr. White about what we could and could not put in its place because of the will and the zoning laws at a later date. The more I thought it over, the more I wanted it built back to its former design. Having an itch to try my hand at farming, I thought of turning it toward herbs, exotic plants, and spices that could be used or sold. Kenrick thought it was leaving negativity on the property and wanted us to put a storage shed or a pit barbeque there but they were just too manly for my liking. If he wanted those, then he could build them in the back between our yard and the neighbor who had the small vineyard in his backyard.

Shoving the door shut, he placed the bag and the crutches at the other end of the sofa for me. I could still reach them but it wasn't in my way if I leaned back and relaxed for a little bit.

"It's time for you to take your meds," he pointed out as he tossed me a bag he'd been hiding in his windbreaker pocket. "I got them filled when I went down to get the car. I hope you're okay with that."

"You seem to keep taking liberties, Mr. Giles," came my straight-faced comment.

"But they're allowed if they are helpful to you, correct? This kept us from having to make another stop as a storm will be rolling in in about an hour. And as it would have had the dose you took earlier wearing off, then you needed to have it before the pain sets in."

"You're smart and have good timing but you still need to ask me before you take over my life."

"Yes, ma'am." He bowed to me and went to get a glass of water to wash down his pigheaded ways and my prescriptions.

After swallowing down the bitter tasting pills, I sank into the cushions and let them take effect over my aches while I picked up rumbling in the distance. Storms were like romance, they could be gentle and renewing, disastrous when the image cleared, or steam as hot as molten glass. My love for this intriguing incubus had tromped through all of them in a matter of days but he remained mine. As the thunder raged closer, Kenrick set my things back to order and had himself settled under my healing leg before it was upon the estate. Just as the atmosphere became electrified, he leaned his long torso down to take my relaxed mouth in a butterfly-inducing kiss. I ran my uninjured hand through his hair and claimed those teasing lips.

When we broke apart, we were breathing heavily as we stared into the power gleaming in both of our amber lit eyes. I saw through the twin reflections of the window glass what magic was still woven into the two of us. Somehow we had become part of the same gleaming stone of power as we lay entwined on the couch and knew that this nap would be much more appealing as our dreams would take us where our exhausted bodies could not. In the land of oblivion, we would reign as a Queen Succubus and King Incubus. Together.

A word from the author...

I'm Georgia-born from Alabama natives, so in essence, I'm related to myself.

I have mercurial witticism and bountiful one-liners that put a smile on most faces.

I love genres from contemporary romance to dark urban fantasy.

I'm also a member of Georgia Romance Writers, plus Romance Writers of America.